CHARLIE

FOXTROT

A Delta Force Unleashed Thriller

Also by J. Robert Kennedy

CHARLIE FOXTROT

A Delta Force Unleashed Thriller

J. ROBERT KENNEDY

This is a work of fiction. Names, characters, places, and incidents are products of the author's imagination. Any resemblance to actual persons, living or dead, is entirely coincidental.

Copyright ©2022 J. Robert Kennedy

ISBN: 9781990418471

First Edition

For Angela Lansbury,
whose portrayal of Jessica Fletcher helped inspire me to become a
writer.

CHARLIE FOXTROT

A Delta Force Unleashed Thriller

"The struggle for democracy and human rights in Burma is a struggle for life and dignity. It is a struggle that encompasses our political, social and economic aspirations."

Aung San Suu Kyi
Imprisoned State Counselor of Myanmar

"Regard your soldiers as your children, and they will follow you into the deepest valleys; look upon them as your own beloved sons, and they will stand by you even unto death."

Sun Tzu

AUTHOR'S NOTE

There is much debate as to whether the country once known as Burma should still be referred to as such, or as Myanmar, the new official name chosen by the military junta in 1989 and recognized by the United Nations though not by all member states including the United States.

This debate will be left to the scholars.

For the sake of clarity, this author has chosen to refer to the country as Myanmar rather than Burma, and the people as Burmese rather than Myanma, as they still refer to themselves as such.

No offense is intended.

PREFACE

Arlington National Cemetery, located in Virginia, across the Potomac River from Washington, D.C., is hallowed ground. It covers over 600 acres and is the final resting place of many of America's heroes, including military and political figures.

It was established during the Civil War, the first burial taking place May 13, 1864, when Private William Henry Christman was laid to rest. As of this writing, over 400,000 men and women have been buried there including former presidents, almost 400 Medal of Honor winners, and countless heroes who fought and died for their country.

The criteria to be met for burial are strict as the space is limited, however, when one of America's heroes dies in the line of duty while fighting his nation's enemies, there is never any doubt of their eligibility.

And today, one more plot will be prepared for a member of America's elite Delta Force, who will make the ultimate sacrifice.

And die a hero, saving one of his brothers-in-arms.

Yangon, Myanmar
Present Day

Sergeant Donald "Sweets" Peters crouched as they took heavy fire. He raised his M4 and squeezed the trigger then glanced over his shoulder to see the civilians crouching against the wall, the Marine embassy guards and the flight crew from the downed Black Hawk covering them with their weapons and physically with their bodies, all willing to take a round should it mean saving the lives of one of those they were here to rescue.

Myanmar's former capital of Yangon had erupted into chaos, and only God knew how many were dead at this point. Hundreds of troops were closing in on their position, and unless they could keep moving, the enemy would zero in on them shortly and all would be lost.

They had to get out of here. Now.

A woman screamed behind him and he spun toward the anguished sound. One of the embassy staffers collapsed to the ground, gripping her shoulder. He rushed to her side and moved her hand away. "Let me take a look at that."

She winced as he ripped her sleeve off, revealing the bullet had passed through and the bleeding was minimal.

"You're going to be fine. Let me just get you bandaged up."

"Are you sure?"

He grabbed his med kit and went to work. "Hey, I'm a pro. You'll be better than new before you know it with a cool story to tell."

She giggled, immediately regretting it. "It better be a damned good story."

"Bring up the eighty!" shouted Master Sergeant Mike "Red" Belme from behind him. Sergeant Eugene "Jagger" Thomas rushed past them with the Carl Gustaf 84-millimeter recoilless rifle as Red took a knee beside the wounded civilian. "Status?"

"She'll live. Through-and-through, nothing major hit." Sweets grinned at her. "But it hurts like a bitch, doesn't it?"

She grunted. "That's about the politest way I'd describe it."

He tightened off the bandage as Jagger fired the 84-millimeter, the resulting explosion shaking the ground and silencing the .50 cal.

Red rose. "Let's get the hell off this—"

Two shots rang out and he went down in a heap, unmoving. Sweets dove toward his fallen comrade and cursed. Two rounds to the chest. He checked for a pulse and found none. He activated his comms.

"Zero-Two is down! I repeat, Zero-Two is down!"

En Route to the American Embassy

Yangon, Myanmar

Present Day, Two Days Earlier

Louise Chambers closed her eyes, pinching the bridge of her nose. She was exhausted, though she wasn't one to feel sorry for herself. As the wife of an ambassador, she had a job to do, and that was to run the household and deal with all the problems that came with doing so in a hostile foreign country like Myanmar. Her husband was good at his job, excellent at it, if his superiors were to be believed, which was why the president had chosen him for what was a shit assignment—they needed an experienced person for a delicate situation.

Myanmar was a horrible country compared to most assignments he was qualified for. It wasn't the people—they were lovely. It was the government. It was a constant struggle for democracy, the experiment having failed, the Sunday morning quarterbacks mistakenly blaming Aung San Suu Kyi for the failure without understanding that the government she had led was never truly democratic, the military continuing to influence things far too freely, including the crackdown on the Rohingya Muslims. Now, she languished in prison because she dared to challenge the generals.

The military was fully in charge once again and things were untenable, the violence escalating with each passing day. It made her husband's job far more difficult and far more dangerous than it should normally be. It also made her life more difficult. All non-essential staff had already been sent back home, and many of the locals were too scared to work and had simply stopped showing up. It meant closing up the official residence had become her responsibility with little assistance, but the job was done despite her husband's insistence it wasn't necessary.

He had wanted her on a plane with all the others, but she was having none of that. Her place was at his side. It always had been. She was the wife of a man in the service of his country. She would never abandon him, especially in stressful times like these—she was the only bit of normalcy left in his life now that the children had families of their own back home.

They were a team.

She leaned her head back against the sumptuous leather of the Lincoln Navigator as her driver, Devon Crane, expertly guided them through the streets of the former capital of this confusing nation, once known as Burma, now Myanmar, the city where the embassies of the nations of the world were located, Yangon, once Rangoon, no longer the capital. The military government had moved the capital to Naypyidaw, a purpose-built city to the north, the jury still out on whether it was a failed experiment.

She opened her eyes and stared out the window at the poverty. There was poverty back home, vicious poverty, but it couldn't compare to this. Millions of people crammed together, most not knowing from where their next meal was coming. She felt terrible for them and had hoped she might do more to help during their tenure here. Unfortunately, all charitable activities ended when the military took back complete control.

She sighed. She was looking forward to going home at the end of his assignment, which couldn't come soon enough. Hopefully, after paying his dues, her husband would be named the ambassador to a much more desirable country where she could do the charity work that she so enjoyed.

"Holy shit!" exclaimed Crane from the driver's seat. She jerked forward as he hammered on the brakes, turning to swerve to their left. A sickening thud was followed by a cry, and her heart leaped into her throat as she recognized it was that of a small child. They came to a shuddering halt, the anti-lock brakes allowing Crane to steer while slowing, but not defy the laws of physics.

She leaned forward, struggling to see what they had hit, and was sickened to see a red bouncing ball come to rest in the gutter on the opposite side of the road. She removed her seatbelt and flung open her door.

"Mrs. Chambers, no!" cried Crane.

But she ignored him. She stepped out into the hot, humid air, and gasped at the sight of a small child, perhaps six years old, lying on the road, a pool of blood forming under her head. Louise rushed forward and dropped to her knees as Crane exited the vehicle, a crowd gathering.

A woman screamed, rushing from a nearby shop. It was clearly someone who knew the little girl, likely her mother.

Louise looked up at her. "I'm so sorry. Let us help."

Crane stepped closer. "Ma'am, we need to get you out of here now."

"We need to help this child."

"Ma'am, there's no helping her."

The woman, now on her knees, held the little girl tight against her chest. She turned her head and screamed something toward the shop she had emerged from moments earlier. A man appeared, his mouth agape, his eyes wide. Louise made eye contact with him and his shock instantly turned to rage. He disappeared inside, reappearing a moment later carrying a large machete, screaming at her as he advanced, fury in his eyes. He charged, the blade held high, and she flinched twice as two shots rang out from behind her. The man collapsed and an iron grip on her arm startled her as Crane hauled her to her feet, dragging her toward their SUV.

The crowd erupted with anger as she was shoved into the back seat and the door slammed shut. More gunshots erupted and Louise's shaking hands struggled with her seatbelt as she watched in horror as the crowd rushed toward Crane. He fired several more rounds, this time into the crowd, and they backed off slightly, allowing him to open the driver's side door and get in. He closed his door and hammered on the gas, pushing through the crowd surrounding them. She clasped her face as the Navigator rocked violently as they ran over bodies.

"Ma'am, are you all right?"

She didn't hear him, the question merely background noise, the chaos that still surrounded them all she could focus on.

"Ma'am, are you all right?" he repeated, this time more forcefully.

She sniffed hard, snapping back to reality. "Y-yes, I think so. Are-are you all right?"

"I will be."

She opened her eyes and finally took notice of her protector and gasped at the bloody gash on his arm. "Oh my God! What happened?"

"One of them got a little too close with a machete."

"We need to get you to a hospital!"

He shook his head. "No, we need to get you to the embassy. That's probably the only safe place for you now until we can get you out of the country."

She stared at him in the rearview mirror. "Is it really that bad?"

"Ma'am, we have diplomatic plates and I saw at least a dozen cameras filming you. They'll have you identified in minutes, and once the government gets their hands on this, they're going to use it against us."

She removed her seatbelt and climbed into the passenger seat.

"You should stay in the back, ma'am. It's safer."

"Nonsense." She removed her scarf, a gift from her husband on her last birthday. She rolled it up then applied it to Crane's wound as a tourniquet.

"Make it tight."

She did and he winced. "Too tight?"

He shook his head. "No, that's good. Now, put your seatbelt on."

9

She sat back and did as told, eying him. "Are you going to be able to get us there or do you want me to drive?"

"No, ma'am. I'll be fine. But in case I'm not, just push me out onto the street and take over."

"I'll do no such thing!"

"Ma'am, you're not strong enough to get me out of this seat."

"Then maybe we should switch now while you still are."

He shook his head. "No. You don't know the streets like I do. If we have to leave the main roads, you could put us down a dead end." He pressed harder on the gas, doing everything with his left hand, his right arm limp at his side. "I'll get you to do one thing for me."

"Anything."

"Lean over here and take the wheel for a second." She did, and using his left hand, he reinserted his comms that had fallen out during the scuffle. "This is Red Rover to Hometown, Red Rover to Hometown. I'm declaring an emergency." He glanced in the rearview mirror and cursed. She spun to see several vehicles pursuing them and finally understood their true predicament.

They hadn't escaped from a violent situation—they were still escaping.

And the moment Crane couldn't drive anymore, they were dead.

"We're coming in hot. ETA, four minutes. We have hostiles in pursuit. Request you be ready to open the gate." Something was said. "Acknowledged, Homefront. I'll be needing medical assistance as well upon arrival. Package is secure and safe, over." He glanced at her. "I'm starting to fade. You know the route?"

10

Her eyes filled with tears as her bottom lip trembled. "Yes, but you hang on. I can't do this without you."

His head drooped then jerked back up and she looked at his arm, his sleeve soaked in blood, the knot she had tied in the tourniquet having come loose.

"Oh, no!" she cried, reaching forward and untying it then resecuring it.

He grunted then removed his hand from the steering wheel for a moment, pressing something. "I've set the cruise control." He turned to her, his voice weak. "Good luck, Mrs. Chambers. It's been a privilege."

He suddenly opened the door and rolled out onto the road. She screamed in horror as she grabbed the wheel. She stared back to see two of the vehicles pursuing them screech to a halt, men pouring out with machetes, and she vomited as they began hacking poor Crane to death. A warning sensor beeped, indicating she was about to hit something. Her head spun back around and she cried out as the vehicle braked to avoid another car directly ahead.

She scrambled into the driver's seat and reached out, grabbing the wildly swinging door, shutting it before making certain it was locked. She cranked the wheel, passing the stationary vehicle that had brought her to a halt, then hammered on the gas. She kept it floored, picking up speed as she repeatedly honked the horn. It took a moment for her to gain her bearings, and she cursed as she realized she had to make a left immediately ahead. She laid on the horn and cranked the wheel at the intersection, her back end fishtailing out and slamming into a parked car.

She floored it again and the Navigator surged forward. She could see the grounds of the embassy ahead and she continued pulsing her horn. A Marine guard rushed out onto the road, waving his arms and directing her into the compound. She took her foot off the gas, checking her rearview mirror to see her pursuers closing in. She hit the brakes, cranking the wheel to the left, and hammered on the accelerator one last time as she surged through the gates and to safety. The Marine rushed in behind her, the gates closing as her pursuers came to a halt, pouring out of their vehicles and rushing the gate. Gunfire rang out as two of the local guards supplied by the Myanmar government opened fire, shooting in the air to disperse the angry crowd.

She continued toward the main building then slammed on the brakes and turned the engine off, slumping against the steering wheel as her entire body was racked with sobs. Somebody knocked hard on the window, startling her, and she jerked back in her seat to see a Marine.

"Unlock your door, Mrs. Chambers."

She eyed the door, looking for the lock. She pressed the button and heard the click. The door opened, the thick air of the coastal city rolling in, competing with the air conditioning.

"Are you injured, ma'am?"

She shook her head. "No, no, but you have to go back for him! They're killing him!" She wailed as she clasped her face. "Oh, my God! He's dead! He's already dead!"

"Louise! My God, what's happened?"

She cried out then climbed down from the Navigator, sprinting full speed into her husband's arms as he rushed out of the building. He held her tight, repeating his question.

"What happened?"

But she couldn't answer, her sobs overwhelming, her entire body shaking violently as her lungs burned. He gently stroked her hair.

"It's all right. You're safe. Take some deep, slow breaths. Calm yourself and tell me what happened."

His voice was soothing, calming, and he was right. She was safe. She inhaled deeply then exhaled, her sobs slowing and she looked up at him. "We hit a little girl. It was an accident. I think she ran out in front of the SUV to get her ball. Devon tried to avoid her but couldn't." She pressed her forehead against his chest. "It's my fault. I was stupid. He tried to stop me but I got out to see if I could help."

"Oh, no, you didn't!"

"I'm so sorry. It's all my fault. They attacked us. He got me inside then someone hit him with a machete in the arm. He got back in and got us out of there, but he lost too much blood. I tried putting a tourniquet on him but I didn't do it properly. Oh God, I'm so sorry. If I had just put it on properly, he'd still be alive."

"You don't know that. Then what happened?"

"He was about to pass out from blood loss. He knew there was no way we could switch seats so I could drive, so he sacrificed himself."

"What do you mean?" Her husband's voice was barely a whisper.

"He opened his door and jumped out. Some of the cars chasing us stopped and the men attacked him with machetes."

"Is he dead?"

"He has to be."

"But you're not sure."

She shook her head. "No, I'm sorry. I'm not."

"Where did this happen?"

She pointed. "Just around the corner. Maybe half a mile back."

Her husband turned. "Tell the locals."

"Yes, sir." Somebody ran off as her husband continued to hold her. She pressed her cheek against him.

"It's all my fault. He sacrificed himself to save me."

"He did his job. Don't blame yourself. Now, let's get you inside and checked out." He helped her up the steps and turned to someone. "Get me Washington on the line. I think we're going to have a situation here. Prep everyone for evac just in case."

"Yes, sir."

She squeezed her eyes shut. A little girl was dead. It was nobody's fault. It was an accident, but she had gotten out of the vehicle against all her training drummed into her since before they arrived. If they were involved in an accident, they were to leave the scene, return to the embassy and report the incident. It was standard procedure, but she had broken the protocol, and because of it, not only was the little girl dead, but so was the man who was likely her father, and everybody else Crane had shot as he fought to get back into the vehicle to save her from her own stupidity. And now Crane was dead as well, saving her. The little girl's death was an accident, but all the rest that followed were avoidable and were all her fault.

She just prayed no more would die because of her foolishness.

Tha Pyae Kone Army Base
Outside Yangon, Myanmar

Captain Champo collapsed backward, landing on a stack of empty pallets, his phone that had just delivered the shocking news still gripped in his hand.

"What's wrong?" asked his best friend since childhood, Kan.

Champo shook his head. "I…" But he was at a loss for words. He handed the phone over and Kan read the message and gasped.

"This can't be true, can it?"

Champo shrugged. "It's from my sister-in-law, Garma. She wouldn't make something like that up."

"But it can't be true. She's saying that the Americans killed your niece and your brother. The Americans are supposed to be the good guys."

Champo hissed at him, holding up a hand. "Keep it down or you're going to get us in trouble."

Kan glanced around for any senior officers. They were both Myanmar army. Champo was a captain and Kan was his lieutenant. He had forty men under his direct command, stationed just outside of Yangon. It was a good job, a good career, and once he had embraced the principles of the military regime, he had been promoted and granted the red scarf. The unit he now led was feared and respected, one of the more brutal deployed to deal with the Rohingya situation several years back.

He didn't embrace all the beliefs. He wasn't a superstitious man like too many of the generals were, but he loved his country and believed in protecting it from its enemies, and that included Muslim extremists. But he never thought it would include Americans. Yes, they were the ideological enemies of Myanmar's current regime, but they were never the enemy of the people.

Until now.

His precious niece Nilar, such a sweet little girl that he had bounced on his knee not ten days ago, was dead by their hands, his brother gunned down. His eyes burned, his chest tightened, a pit of rage forming in his stomach. He squeezed his eyes shut and clenched his fists.

They had to pay.

He sniffed hard, feeding off his rage and burying the sorrow. Grieving would come later. He had a job to do and Americans to kill. He pushed to his feet and took back the phone, sending a text message to his sister-in-law.

They will be avenged.

Behind 1st Special Forces Operational Detachment—Delta HQ

Fort Bragg, North Carolina

A.k.a. "The Unit"

"Fine, I'll take a stab at it. Bridget Jones' Diary, James Blunt, and Pride and Prejudice."

Command Sergeant Major Burt "Big Dog" Dawson chomped down on what might possibly be the best hamburger he had ever tasted. Vanessa Moore, who had just given her answer to which movie, album, and book you would choose if stranded on a desert island for the rest of your life, was an exceptional chef. To call her a cook would put her in the same classification as him, and there was no way what she did in a kitchen and what he did were remotely similar.

Every hamburger patty was handmade with a mix of spices and seasoning that resulted in a burst of flavor. Too often these days, the patty was forgotten. Burgers were topped with endless combinations of ingredients that overpowered the beef. While he had no doubt Vanessa was capable of making a burger that foodies would write articles about, she knew her audience. She was cooking for soldiers, for grunts, for a bunch of NCOs who loved their meat, especially when it was barbecued.

They were 1st Special Forces Operational Detachment—Delta, more commonly known to the public as the Delta Force, and they had just come off two back-to-back missions. Everyone was tired but happy. He personally loved going out on missions, especially like the last one where the outcome was so satisfying and they had made a true difference. But there was nothing like coming home to family, coming back to the Unit he called home. Bravo Team, of which he was the leader, was gathered with their families behind the Unit, chowing down on burgers and salads, and sipping on a few cold ones. It was bliss, and there was no place he would rather be.

Vanessa's boyfriend, the ridiculously muscled Sergeant Leon "Atlas" James, chuckled in his equally ridiculously deep voice. "I think you just stole Niner's answers."

The diminutive by comparison Sergeant Carl "Niner" Sung flipped the big man the bird. "Shows what you know."

"Oh, and what would you have chosen?"

Niner's head lolled to the side toward his girlfriend, Angela Henwood. "Care to guess?"

Her eyebrows shot up. "Are you kidding me? We've only been dating a few months."

He shrugged. "Humor me."

"Fine, based upon what I've seen, Notting Hill, anything by BTS, and Little Women."

Niner stared at her aghast, his mouth agape as everyone roared with laughter.

Atlas stabbed a finger at him. "That is *so* you."

"That is *so* not! Tell them, honey, you're just making that up!"

She shrugged, her expression all innocence. "I can only go by what I've seen."

Niner groaned. "I should have known, you guys have corrupted her. You've turned her against me."

Red, Dawson's best friend and second-in-command, shrugged. "It was bound to happen eventually. Anyone who gets to know you discovers your true nature."

Sergeant Will "Spock" Lightman cocked an eyebrow. "And just what is his true nature?"

Vanessa pointed at Niner with a metal spatula. "That his one true love is Atlas?"

More laughter had some of the children rushing over, demanding an explanation for why their parents were laughing so hard. None was provided, but that didn't prevent them from laughing, if not with their parents, then at them.

Niner leaned over and patted Atlas on the leg, a little too high up the inner thigh for the big man's liking. "It's true. I gave him my heart but he sucker punched it, and instead decided to date some woman just because she was a good cook."

Atlas squeezed Vanessa's hand. "It wasn't because you're a good cook."

"I should hope not."

"It was your booty."

"That's better." She gave Atlas a kiss then flipped the burgers she was tending. "So, my dear, what would *your* three choices be?"

"Easy. The Hangover, because I get to see Niner jump out of the trunk of a car naked revealing his tiny dangler, anything by my man Barry White because he's got a voice almost as deep as mine, and then any mission report where I had to save the little one's ass."

Niner shrugged off the insults. "See, he's obsessed with me. If that's not true love, I don't know what is."

Dawson's phone rang and he fished it out of his shorts, frowning at the call display. It was the Unit. He rose and walked away from the conversation as he took the call. "Hello?"

"Hello, Sergeant Major. Are you still at your barbecue?"

It was Colonel Thomas Clancy, their commanding officer. "Yes, sir."

"I need you to step inside. We have a situation developing in Myanmar."

"I'll be there in five minutes, sir."

"Very well."

The call ended and Dawson headed back to the group. He jerked a thumb over his shoulder at their HQ. "Colonel wants to see me." He waved a finger at his men. "No more beers. We could be deploying."

Jagger thrust his massive lips out in a pout. "Three missions in a week? Who do they think we are?"

Niner leaped to his feet, jamming his fists on his hips. "We're supermen!"

Atlas snorted. "Yeah, I could see you sporting a pair of tights."

Niner gave him a look. "So, you like picturing me in tights, do you?"

Angela snickered and patted Niner's ass. "I don't know about him, but I'm game."

"You'll be my Lois, I'll be your Superman?"

Dawson gave his fiancée Maggie Harris a kiss. "I'll be back in a bit." He jogged over to the main entrance then briskly marched down the corridor toward Clancy's office, his Bermuda shorts and Hawaiian shirt clashing with the crisp fatigues and uniforms worn by most of the admin staff. Operators like him were often in civilian attire, beards and long hair common among Delta, so he was accustomed to standing out while in-country.

He entered the outer office, usually manned by Maggie, but it was the weekend so she had it off. Clancy normally took it off as well and Dawson was surprised he was in. Dawson headed for the inner office and poked his head inside, rapping on the doorframe. "You wanted to see me, Colonel?"

Clancy directed him to a chair in front of his desk, a pen gripped between his fingers replacing the cigars he once habitually smoked. "Have a seat, Sergeant Major. Sorry to interrupt your barbecue. How many beers have you had?"

"Halfway through my second, sir. I'm fine."

"Good. We've got a situation developing in Myanmar that looks like it could turn into a Charlie Foxtrot."

"What's happened, sir?"

"Apparently, the ambassador's wife was returning to the embassy from the official residence when her driver struck a young child."

Dawson frowned. "Let me guess, they didn't follow protocol?"

"She didn't, no. She got out to try to help. They were attacked by the girl's father. The driver took him out along with two others. He ended up getting critically wounded and sacrificed himself to save Mrs. Chambers. She managed to make it back to the embassy, but the driver is dead, hacked to pieces. Myanmar authorities are claiming the two of them killed eleven people and they're demanding she be handed over to stand trial."

"Ignoring diplomatic immunity once again, are they?"

"You know that regime. There isn't a law they wouldn't break if it suited their purposes."

"Weren't they already drawn down?"

"They were. All non-essential personnel were sent home a few months ago. Now the government's whipping things up and they've got thousands out front of the embassy protesting. This could turn into another Tehran if we're not careful."

"We can't have that. What's the mission?"

"Bravo Team's been specifically requested. I guess you're still in the administration's good books."

"A blessing and a curse."

Clancy chuckled. "True. I realize this will be three ops in a week. If you don't feel you're up to it, I'll turn down the request and assign another team."

Dawson shook his head. "No, we can handle it. That last op had big consequences, but only took a day out of our lives."

Clancy regarded him. "A lot of good was done in that one day."

"Yes, sir. A lot of good. When do we ship out?"

"Two hours. Embassy security is attempting to get the bulk of the personnel out tonight under cover of darkness, but a group, including the ambassador, is remaining behind to throw off the locals. If the embassy went dark, they'd know something is up."

"So, our mission is to get the ambassador and the rest of them out?"

"Yes, with the understanding that the entire damn country's going to know what happened the night before by the time you arrive."

Dawson sighed. "Sir, have you ever gone on a mission where you just knew it was going to be a Charlie Foxtrot before you even had boots on the ground?"

Clancy chuckled. "Once or twice, Sergeant Major. Once or twice."

Embassy of the United States of America

Yangon, Myanmar

Jennifer Fawcett gripped the arms of her chair, her eyes closed, her chin tilted up, as Bennu, one of the local hires, applied the *thanaka* makeup to her cheeks. Ambassador Nick Chambers entered the room and Jennifer began to stand.

He waved her off and smiled. "You look like a local."

"That's the idea, sir. Hopefully, it'll fool people long enough for us to get to the airport."

"Hopefully." He addressed Bennu. "And what's that stuff called again?"

"It's called thanaka, sir. It's meant to beautify and protect the skin. It's been used by my people for thousands of years." Bennu stepped back. "You're ready."

Jennifer rose and stared at herself in the mirror. "Well, I don't know if I'll pass as a local. I'm half a foot taller than most women here."

Chambers smiled. "Hunch over. At this hour, there shouldn't be too many people out anyway."

Jennifer turned to Bennu. "Are you going to be all right?"

Bennu nodded. "We'll be fine. As soon as you're clear, we're all crossing the lake then heading home."

Chambers extended a hand and clasped Bennu's. "You take care of yourself and pass that on to the rest of the staff. We appreciate everything you've done for us. Just go home. If anyone asks, you quit because of what happened. When we come back, we'll let you know and you can decide whether you want to return to your job."

"Thank you, Ambassador. I'll be praying for all of you."

Chambers beckoned Jennifer to follow him and they were soon in the rear courtyard, out of sight from those still protesting outside. The numbers might have lowered slightly due to the hour, but there were still thousands out front. Fortunately, the embassy backed on Inya Lake, where few, if any, of the angry eyes were focused. The bulk of the remaining embassy staff were gathered along with most of their Embassy Guard. Everyone was dressed in local attire—Western-style business garb would stand out too much with what was going on, especially at this time of night.

She had never really felt uncomfortable during her entire assignment here, though you always had to be smart. Like in most major cities, as a woman, she never went out alone at night. But during the day, she always felt comfortable leaving the embassy grounds to grab lunch at a local shop. The locals were extremely friendly, and you simply didn't make eye contact with any of the soldiers, especially those wearing red scarves.

But since yesterday's events, she had been terrified. She was putting on the brave face expected of her position, determined not to be a liability and to be a role model to everyone, men and women alike, despite her fervent wish to curl up into a ball somewhere and hide. A small child had died. It had been an accident, but the aftermath had resulted in far more deaths.

The military junta was claiming eleven people had died, shot by Mrs. Chambers and her driver as they attempted to escape their crime. It was bullshit, of course, though there was no doubt several people had been shot and killed in self-defense. Governments like this had a habit of grossly inflating anything that they could link to a kernel of truth. "See, there's one body. Why won't you believe me when I say there are ten more?" They were demanding that Louise be handed over to stand trial, which was a violation of international law, but the law meant little to those who ruled this country, once again overthrowing the democratic will of the people.

Sergeant Major Martinez, in charge of the Marine Embassy Guard, held up a hand and the murmured conversations stopped. He beckoned everyone closer then spoke in a harsh whisper. "We're about to leave. It's essential that everyone keeps absolutely quiet. Right now, there's no evidence that anyone out front knows what we're about to do. We've managed to secure three vehicles and they're parked on the other side of the lake waiting for us. Unfortunately, we can only accommodate twelve people and it's going to be tight. I have a list of names that I'm going to read off, people with known medical conditions or mobility issues. Those people have been assigned slots in those vehicles because they might not be able to make it to the airport on foot."

Everyone looked about, wondering who would get lucky. She was certain she wouldn't. She was healthy and could walk or run should it become necessary, but there were others in the group nearing retirement, and she was aware of others with bad knees or hips, and a few who were frankly too overweight and out of shape should they be required to run.

Ambassador Chambers walked up as the murmuring among the group threatened to get too loud. "This list is final. Nobody asked to be on it. It was all decided by the doctor and me. If you're on the list and you don't want to be on the list, too bad, you're on the list and you're getting in one of those cars. You may think you're not a liability and quite possibly you're not, but if something goes wrong, the group is only as fast as its slowest member and your pride now could cost lives later." He held up a finger. "And for that same reason, nobody is to make anybody feel guilty about being on that list." He turned to Martinez. "Go ahead, Sergeant Major."

Martinez pointed toward the gated entrance that led to the pedestrian bridge built to cross to the east side of the lake. "If I say your name, wait by the gate." He read off nine names, some of them gasping in shock that they were on the list, a few clearly putting on a show, including Marsha Doyle, a large woman who was one of the sweetest people she had ever met and her regular lunch companion.

Marsha turned to the others. "I'm so sorry. I'm really so sorry." Tears flowed down the woman's cheeks and Jennifer stepped forward and embraced her.

"You have nothing to be sorry about."

Marsha sniffed. "Thank you. Thank you for always being so kind and for never judging me."

Jennifer gave her another squeeze. "It's time for you to go. I'll see you on the plane."

Marsha sniffed again. "All right, I'll see you soon. Good luck to you all." She headed over to the gate, some of her fellow staff members comforting her, others glaring as they judged her for what too many felt was a conscious choice. Obesity was the one thing society still accepted discrimination against. Creed, color, religion, sexual orientation, were all now taboo. But if someone was fat, whether in the movies, TV shows, or memes on the Internet, it was still open season, as it was here tonight with daggers shot at Marsha as she winced her way toward the gate. Her knees were a source of constant agony since she was a child, long before she had put on a pound, yet her mobility issues were blamed on her weight by all the armchair experts now staring at her, no one considering it could be the other way around.

The nine were now gathered by the gate and the ambassador addressed the remaining group. "If there's anyone who feels they should be included in that group, there are three slots left, so if you've been hiding something from the doctor because you didn't want it on the official record, speak up now."

At least a dozen hands shot up.

"I tweaked my knee yesterday!" yelled Steven Heinz, and everyone glared at him.

"Keep your voice down!" snapped Martinez. He pointed at the doctor standing nearby. "Anybody who thinks they should be on that list, talk to the doctor. His say is final." He pointed at the gate. "When we get to the other side of the lake, we'll be splitting into two groups. Those going to the cars, continue straight on with the three Marine escorts who will be your drivers. The rest will turn north and follow me as quietly as possible. We'll be heading for the airport. It's six miles away. We'll be walking at a brisk pace, and if all goes well, we should be there in well under two hours. If something goes wrong, do not engage. Follow the orders of your escort and make sure you have your diplomatic passports handy so that you can hold them up. Be prepared to run, though." Martinez turned to the doctor. "Is the list final?"

"Yes, it is." The doctor pointed at three of the staffers, including Heinz who smiled then headed for the gate with a limp that Jennifer was certain hadn't been there before.

"Asshole," she muttered.

"Coward is more like it," said Rick Burman, one of the newer staffers. "I hope he catches a stray bullet for faking it."

The gates swung open and everyone fell silent. Two Marines led the way and were soon lost in the dark. The twelve lucky souls assigned to the vehicles slowly filed through and Marsha turned back and gave her a weak wave. Jennifer gave her a reassuring smile and returned the wave, blowing her a kiss before her friend turned and stepped onto what in the United States would never be called a bridge. It was a makeshift creation of bamboo and rope that many of the local hires used to bypass the front gate and its government observers, and would have been dismantled by the authorities back home as a hazard.

The rest gathered, the ambassador and his wife wishing everyone good luck as they filed past. Her pulse pounded in her ears as she passed through the gate and took her first tentative step onto the bridge that would hopefully lead to their salvation. It wasn't very long, but it also wasn't very wide, which had everyone going far slower than they might have in the light of day and when nerves weren't so frayed. The incessant chanting from the front of the embassy seemed louder here, though it was probably just her imagination. The bridge was bouncing with a horrible creaking that continued to get worse, accompanied by the occasional snap.

Somebody yelped and at least two dozen people responded with "Shhh."

"Sorry," was the meek reply as the snapping continued.

"There are too many of us," she whispered harshly. A loud snap was followed by a collective gasp as the entire bridge jerked.

"Everyone freeze," hissed someone ahead. She stopped, her heart racing as if she were at the end of a three-mile run. The bridge continued to sway though it eased up slightly. "One at a time," said the voice ahead and she peered into the darkness, most of the light provided by the moon and stars overhead. Large trees shielded them from the streetlights on the road that ran in front of the embassy and prevented, she hoped, those who wanted their heads from seeing them.

She spotted movement ahead. There were perhaps ten people between her and the front of the line. She glanced behind her, at least another ten or fifteen still waiting. This was taking too long. There were residences within sight. All it would take would be for someone to look out the wrong window and catch sight of them, or for one of their group to be overheard. Impatient muttering grew in intensity. After what felt like an eternity but was only minutes, it was her turn. She took each step carefully, the bridge still wobbling, tilting violently to the left near the midpoint where the ropes had snapped from the strain of so many people.

Her feet slipped and one of those at the far end whispered, "Take the high side."

She did as told and struggled not to panic as she continued to slip, though this time with plenty of room to correct herself before she went into the water. She kept pushing forward. It was only one more foot until the bridge straightened back out, but the shoes she had chosen, while comfortable because they were well-worn, also included well-worn soles. It had never occurred to her that she'd need grip like this—she just didn't want blisters from the long walk ahead.

Both feet slipped and she tumbled to her side. Her instinct said to shout out but she clamped her jaw shut. She wouldn't be the death of them all. Her hip smacked into the hard bamboo and she winced. Her hand darted out, gripping a raised edge as her feet slid in the water. She finally steadied herself then raised her free hand. "I'm all right," she whispered. She pushed up to her knees then crawled the rest of the way to the level portion of the bridge, then unsteadily rose to her feet.

She made it the rest of the way across then sighed heavily in relief as she stepped onto solid ground, taking the extended hand of a Marine as he helped her the last few feet. She glanced back to see the next person behind her dropping to his knees and crawling over the dangerous portion with relative ease, and perhaps her unfortunate accident could save them all from another louder mishap.

The Marine sergeant pointed at one of his comrades. "Check out her leg."

"Huh?"

He pointed and she looked down to see blood on the traditional robe she was wearing. The other Marine beckoned her over and he dropped to his knees. "Forgive me, ma'am." He raised the wrap so he could see her upper thigh. "Looks like you have a shard of bamboo stuck in here. I'm going to remove it. Bite down on your finger. Make sure you don't cry out."

She did as told and he carefully pulled the sliver out, the experience agonizing.

"This is going to sting." He poured something over the wound and she gasped, a string of curses erupting that her mother would have slapped her for. The Marine snickered as he started wrapping the wound.

"I think I learned some new ones there, ma'am."

"Glad to help. Just don't give me any credit. I'm liable to get demoted."

He patted her leg. "How does that feel?"

She lifted her leg, bending it at the knee. "It'll get me where I need to go."

"Try walking on it."

She took a few tentative steps. It hurt a bit but she'd manage.

"Are you good?"

She grunted. "It's not like I have a choice now, do I?"

"I'm afraid not, ma'am. But if you have any trouble, you let one of us know. We'll carry you out if we have to."

She chuckled. "If I had known that was an option, I would've volunteered at the start of the bridge."

He smiled. "Careful, you might just get what you wish for."

She slapped his arm. "Get back to work, Corporal. I'll be fine." She joined the others gathering along the shore, some of them watching the slow progress of the crossing, the rest staring uneasily into the night. She surveyed their surroundings, struggling to calm her out-of-control heart. Several boats were tied up nearby, and she wondered why they weren't using them. They could easily fit half their number, and two trips would have everyone to the northern tip of the lake, far closer to the airport.

She turned to Rick, gesturing at the three moored vessels. "Shouldn't we be taking the boats?"

He glanced over at them then firmly shook his head. "No, that's a recipe for disaster."

She bristled at the quick dismissal. "How so?"

"Well, just look at them. They're not in very good condition, and if one of them were to sink or capsize, there's no way we could keep that quiet, especially considering probably half the people here don't know how to swim, not to mention the fact that all of them have outboard motors. As soon as we started one of them, this whole neighborhood would be awake. We're better off on foot."

A bright light suddenly shone on them and everyone spun to find the source.

And Jennifer cursed as a woman she recognized holding a microphone stared at them.

Inya Lake, Eastern Shore

Yangon, Myanmar

Aynslee Kai cursed and turned back, waving a hand at her cameraman. "Shut the damn light off. Are you trying to get everybody killed?"

The camera angled down toward the ground and the light flicked off. "Sorry about that. Habit."

"Just use the night filter."

Neville Roy adjusted the camera settings then hoisted it back on his shoulder. Aynslee turned back to the group. She had been in Indonesia covering a G20 conference and was about to head home to New York when word of what had happened in Myanmar reached her. She had been looking for an excuse to get inside the country ruled once again by the repressive regime, and arrangements had been made by her producers. Last-minute credentials had been granted when the producers made it clear to the Myanmar media relations people that she intended to cover both sides of the story, insisting on interviewing a government spokesperson and, if possible, the mother.

She had interviewed the government mouthpiece and a few clips from it might be used. The interview with the mother had been heartbreaking. There was genuine grief, genuine loss—there was no faking what she was saying or feeling. She had lost her daughter and husband, though the husband only had himself to blame. Interviews with neighbors suggested that two other people had been killed by the driver in addition to the father, despite the insistence of their government escort that eleven had been killed. She had requested permission to view the bodies but that had been refused. They were willing to show her the little girl, but that was it. She had turned down their offer. There was no reason to broadcast something like that.

The poor thing had been through enough already and didn't deserve to be used as a pawn in her death.

They had shaken their escort at the hotel, telling the man they were in for the night, and as soon as he had been spotted leaving, they had hurried over to the embassy. Roy had spotted the activity at the rear of the compound when he had climbed to the second floor of a nearby building for a better shot of the crowds. They had made their way through a posh neighborhood east of the compound, then stumbled on what was clearly an escape attempt.

She held her microphone to her mouth. "I'm Aynslee Kai, CNN. Can you please confirm that you are embassy staff?"

A Marine corporal rushed over, placing himself between her and the others, all dressed in local attire. "Ma'am, you can't be here."

"Actually, I can. It's a little thing called freedom of the press."

"And if we were on American soil, that would be true, but we're not. And you're here without an escort, which tells me you're not allowed to be here. But more importantly, ma'am, you're putting all these people's lives at risk."

"That's not my intention. All I ask is that we be allowed to ask some questions."

A sergeant major marched up. "What the hell is going on here?" he hissed. "I can hear you clear across the bridge."

The corporal snapped to attention. "Sergeant Major, a CNN crew has discovered us."

The sergeant major glared at her. "Please tell me you're not inconsiderate enough to be broadcasting live?"

Aynslee shook her head. "Of course not. We're just here to do our job."

He squinted at her in the darkness. "You're Aynslee Kai, aren't you?"

"I am."

"I recognize you. Well, you may have a job to do, but so do I, and that's to get all these people through hostile territory to an evac point six miles away without being discovered. Your presence makes that all the more difficult." He turned to the corporal. "Everyone's across. Get them moving."

"Yes, Sergeant Major." The corporal headed off and the sergeant major returned his attention to her.

"I don't have time to deal with you, but you two in your western clothes with a camera and a microphone stand out like sore thumbs among this group, all of whom are disguised as locals. You're going to draw too much attention. So, what's it going to be?"

Aynslee watched as the group of men and women shuffled by, terror in their eyes. The women had the makeup of the locals on their cheeks, and it was clear significant effort had gone into the disguises. And the sergeant major was right. She and her cameraman did not fit in with this group. If someone caught sight of the escapees, they might not give them a second glance. But if they spotted Roy with his camera on his shoulder and her with a microphone, that second glance would be merited, and the alarm sounded.

She sighed. "You're right, Sergeant Major. I have a job to do, and so do you, but right now yours is more important than mine." She pointed at the bridge they had been crossing. "Can I assume that leads to the embassy?"

"Yes."

"If we were to cross, will we be allowed in?"

The sergeant major shrugged. "It's worth a shot."

She smiled. "I suppose that's one way of looking at it. Good luck, Sergeant Major. To all of you."

He gave her a crisp nod. "Thank you, ma'am, and thank you for understanding." He did an abrupt left turn, marching rapidly toward the head of the column, and Aynslee pointed at it.

"Make sure you get some good shots of that."

Roy redirected the camera at the departing group and Aynslee had to wonder if this was the last time they would ever be seen by a friendly face. Six miles in New York City was nothing, but six miles here, where everyone thought you were harboring the murderer of a child, might as well be a thousand.

North of University Avenue Road

Yangon, Myanmar

Marsha Doyle climbed into the front seat of the car, her chest heaving as she gasped for breath, her lungs filling with fluid. Three of her colleagues climbed into the back seat and one of their Marine escorts, Corporal Dell, climbed behind the wheel. He started the engine and glanced over at her.

"Are you going to be all right?"

"Don't you worry about me, you just get us to that airport."

"Yes, ma'am."

They pulled away as she continued to suck in air. She had been determined to not slow anybody up, and she hadn't. She had managed to keep pace with the person in front of her. That's all she had promised herself. Just keep pace with the person in front, then she couldn't be blamed for anything. But she had overdone it. Her knees were screaming in agony, her lungs were burning, and she was battling the betrayal of her body. She coughed, phlegm filling her mouth. She swallowed and took a long drink of the water bottle she had been issued.

Just keep it together a little while longer. We'll be on that plane soon. Just keep it together. You don't want to be the reason these people die.

She cursed herself. She had always known her weight was a problem, but it was something she had been suffering from her entire life. She tried every diet, every pill. Nothing worked. Her knees had been shot since she was a child, the cartilage mostly gone. It meant she always had a hard time walking and could never run. Treadmills, bikes, ellipticals, everything, were brutal, agonizing experiences. She had resigned herself to the fact she would be like this for the rest of her life, and that life would be far shorter than it should be.

But that was *her* fate.

Her condition was never meant to decide the fate of others, yet now it was threatening the lives of her colleagues, her friends. She squeezed her eyes shut as the tears flowed and she made a deal with God.

If you get me through this, I swear I'll never leave home again.

God just needed to get her through this, get them all through this, then she would sacrifice her entire future so she would never again put someone's life at risk because of her weight.

A hand gently squeezed her shoulder from the back seat.

"I'm sorry!" she cried out as she flinched.

"Sorry for what?"

She continued to gasp for breath, each word punctuated by a tortured inhalation. "I'm putting all of you at risk." She had to stop talking. She had to focus on her breathing. She recognized the signs of an anxiety attack beginning, which would only exacerbate things.

"Just breathe. We're all safe. You didn't slow us down. If anything, I did. Just focus on my voice. Everybody's calm, everybody's safe. The corporal here is going to have us at the airport in no time, then we'll be on that plane and soon we'll be flying home. They'll have oxygen on that plane, won't they, Corporal?"

"Absolutely, sir. Medics and med kits."

"You hear that? Just slowly calm yourself, and in a few minutes you'll be sucking back on sweet sweet oxygen."

She giggled for the first time since this ordeal began. She relaxed slightly. He was right. She hadn't held them up, and this wasn't her fault. The torture she had suffered since she was a child wasn't because she had done something wrong, it was just the life God had chosen for her. Had she turned to food as a means of escape from her misery? Yes, there was no denying that. Some smoked, some drank, some did drugs.

She ate.

Of the four vices, she had to think food was the lesser of those evils. She inhaled deeply, finally feeling the air reaching the top of her lungs, signaling the beginning of the end of her attack. She reached up and gripped the hand still on her shoulder. "Thank you. I think I'm going to be okay now." Her breathing continued to steady, and the others in the back seat reached forward and patted her on the arm.

"You've got this."

Her breathing steadied, the burn in her lungs subsiding, though she sensed she'd be coughing up fluid for the next several weeks. It wouldn't be the first time, but one of these days would be the last, and her suffering and loneliness would finally be over.

Dell cursed and the car slowed as he took his foot off the gas, gently applying the brakes. She opened her eyes to see what had him concerned, and what she saw triggered her panic anew.

A roadblock.

Pedestrian Path, Eastern Shore of Inya Lake

Yangon, Myanmar

Jennifer Fawcett had given up wincing with every step, and instead simply maintained the facial expression as Sergeant Major Martinez, at the head of the group, set a brutally brisk pace. She had managed to keep pace so far with the group as a whole, but was slowly falling back. They were making good time as they skirted the lake along a walking path she had enjoyed on many occasions, though never at this time of night. They hadn't encountered anybody yet, which was a minor miracle, though perhaps people were staying indoors because of what was happening back at the embassy, or perhaps at the head of the group they were running into people and they were scattering at the sight of the armed Marines. Whatever the reason for their continued success, she didn't care. Every step brought them closer to salvation and every step meant one less left that she'd have to suffer.

The column came to a halt and she pushed up on her toes, searching for a reason why. They were at the tip of the lake now and about to enter a residential district. This was where they could be caught.

The Marine corporal who had bandaged her up joined them from the rear, whispering the instructions that were no doubt being given at the head of the column. "We're about to enter a populated area and it's going to remain that way until we reach the airfield. Stay calm. Stay quiet. We've already covered a mile. We'll be there soon enough." The corporal walked over to her, gesturing at the leg. "How are you doing?"

"It hurts but I'll manage."

"I've noticed you slowing down but you're not holding us up yet. The good news is the rest of the way is going to be slower. So hopefully you'll find it a little easier to keep up."

"Slower?" asked somebody, a little too loudly.

The corporal glared at him. "What did I just say about keeping quiet?"

"Sorry."

"We need to check each road we cross to make sure there's nobody watching. It's going to slow things down."

The column moved again and the corporal gestured for them to get going before returning to his position at the rear. She cringed with the first step then got back into a rhythm. The brisk pace continued for a couple of minutes before they came to an abrupt halt, and she stared ahead to see they were about to cross their first street.

This was where it became dangerous.

The front of the group moved and she readied herself. She reached the curb. Two Marines were covering the street, the sergeant major on the other side, waving them forward. She jogged across, gasping every time the foot of her injured leg made contact with the road. She cleared the street, disappearing into an alleyway with the others, then doubled over, gripping her leg as she shuffled forward to make room for the rest coming behind her, though they were few as she had dropped to almost the back of the pack. She waited as the last of the group cleared the road.

The sergeant major took one final look then headed back toward the front. He stopped beside her. "How's that leg doing?"

She decided honesty was the best policy in this situation. Lying could put people at risk. "Not great. Every step hurts."

"Do you think you can keep up if we keep stopping like this?"

"Yes."

"If you run into trouble, talk to the corporal." He addressed those around her. "Everybody keep your eyes open for something that could be used as a walking stick. It'll help take some of the pressure off her leg."

Heads bobbed around her as everyone took a look. The sergeant major headed back to the front and they were soon underway again. They reached the next street and Jennifer prepared for another rush when a collective gasp swept through them at a sound to their right.

Gunfire.

Kabar Aye Pagoda Road
Yangon, Myanmar

Marsha screamed and squeezed her eyes shut as bullets tore into the hood of the car. She raised her hands in a useless attempt to shield herself from any strays that might make it through the windshield.

"Everybody just remain calm," said Corporal Dell, his voice remarkably steady for one so young.

Marsha wasn't quite sure how to remain calm, having never heard gunfire so close before. It was far louder than anything she imagined, and that, combined with the bullets impacting the metal of the car and the engine block, was simply too much. Her chest tightened and she gasped for breath. The comforting hands from those in the back were gone. She forced her eyes open to see four soldiers standing in front of the vehicle, their weapons aimed directly at them, one of them shouting, gesturing with the muzzle of his rifle for them to get out of the car.

"What do we do?" she asked, her voice trembling.

"We just stay calm," said Dell. "I'm going to get out and show him my ID. Nobody does anything unless I tell you." He slowly reached for the door handle and pulled on it. He pushed the door open then cautiously stepped out, raising his hands. "My name is Corporal Dell. I'm a member of the United States Embassy Security detail. I'm escorting these American citizens who are all embassy staff with diplomatic passports to the airport."

The man apparently in charge wasn't impressed at the fact English was spoken, and he continued to shout at Dell, getting increasingly agitated.

"Maybe we should get out," she said.

"No, you heard what he said. We stay in the car."

Her heart slammed and she was certain she was about to have a heart attack. This had to stop. They weren't doing anything wrong. They were in this country with no restrictions. They had proper identification. They were heading to the airport escorted by Marines also here legally, all with licenses that allowed them to carry their weapons in the execution of duties.

She roared in frustration and threw open her door, struggling to get out of the vehicle. She finally managed to do so, then produced her passport as she leaned heavily on the roof of the car and the door frame. "We are American citizens traveling under diplomatic passports! We are all registered with your government, and it is against the law for you to prevent us from moving freely."

The man glared at her, jabbing a finger at her. "You spies!"

Finally, some English. It meant there might be a way to communicate.

"We're not spies. What would make you say something like that?"

"You dress like Myanmar woman! You spy!"

The man was right. They were dressed as locals to hide the fact they weren't. It had nothing to do with being a spy and everything to do with self-preservation. Unfortunately, he did have reason to be suspicious. She forced a laugh and pointed at her face.

"It was a goodbye party. Our local staffers threw us a party before we left, and to honor them, we all dressed like them."

"You spy!" He raised his weapon at her and she closed her eyes, silently saying goodbye to a life of suffering. Gunfire erupted and her chest squeezed like a vise. She collapsed on the pavement, smacking her head hard as more gunfire erupted around her.

She should have stayed home.

She should have kept her crippled self locked inside.

She should have stayed in New Mexico where she belonged, hidden away where she couldn't hurt anyone.

I'm so sorry.

Sergeant Major Martinez lowered his weapon and cursed at the aftermath of what had just happened. He and two of his men had split off from the group on foot and headed toward the gunfire, one of the drivers radioing in the situation. The mini convoy had been stopped at a roadblock and an overzealous guard had emptied a mag into the engine compartment of the lead vehicle.

It meant five people were about to be on foot, regardless of how this turned out.

50

They had double-timed it to the roadblock, reaching it just as things were about to get out of hand. A large woman shouted at the guards, triggering exactly the type of response one should expect in Myanmar. The man she was arguing with raised his weapon and fired, triggering the response permitted by Martinez's Rules of Engagement.

He and the rest of his men opened fire, taking out all four soldiers. He rushed forward, glancing at the engine compartment of the lead car. It was toast. He rapped on the rear window. "Everybody out!" He continued to the second car. The corporal had his window down and leaned out.

"Sergeant Major, thank God you're here!"

"Lead car's a write-off. We might have one dead." He checked the back seat. "Could you fit one more back here?"

A woman held up her hand. "I can sit in someone's lap."

"Good."

One of the men squeezed into the corner as far as he could and helped the woman into his lap. The third passenger shoved all the way over.

"We can definitely fit one more, maybe even two back here."

"Good work." Martinez stood straight and pointed at two of the passengers in the written-off car. "You two, get in here now."

They hurried toward him, tears streaming down their cheeks. The man got in first, then the woman followed, half-sitting, half-lying across the others.

Martinez slammed the door shut. "It's not going to be comfortable, but you'll be alive. Corporal, get them to the airport, and for the love of God stay inside the car. Don't provoke the locals."

"Yes, Sergeant Major." The corporal pulled away, guiding them around the stricken vehicle and through the roadblock. He gunned the engine and was out of sight within moments as Martinez assessed the rear seat of the third vehicle. He pointed at the lone remaining passenger still standing outside. "Get in the back. Corporal, you know what to do. Get them to the airport, and I can't emphasize this enough, people, stay in the car and don't provoke the locals."

The third backseat passenger from the first vehicle squeezed into the rear seat and they were soon underway. Martinez joined his team assessing the large woman. "What's her status?"

Corporal Dell, her driver, looked up. "Her name's Marsha, Sergeant Major. She took a round to the chest."

"Is she going to make it?"

"Right side. She's having trouble breathing, but she had trouble earlier. I think she's prone to panic attacks."

Martinez took a knee beside her. "Ma'am, how do you feel?"

Dell shook his head. "She's out cold. Hit her head pretty hard. Might have a concussion."

"Damn it to hell." He surveyed the area. The woman was large, certainly over three bills. If they had a stretcher, four men could carry her all the way to the airport, though it would be difficult and it would take time. But it was time the woman didn't have. She needed medical attention and the only places she could get it were back at the embassy or at the airport where their plane would be landing soon with highly trained medics and supplies just for such an eventuality.

He spotted a military jeep nearby and made a judgment call. He pointed at one of his men. "Go check and see if you can get that thing running."

"Yes, Sergeant Major."

The sergeant rushed off and Martinez stood. "Can she be moved?"

"She probably shouldn't be, but I don't think we have a choice, do we?"

"No, we don't."

The engine roared to life and the sergeant soon had the jeep beside Marsha.

"Okay, everybody, let's get her in the back seat."

The four of them struggled to lift the dead weight and finally got her in the back seat and strapped in.

"Sergeant, you get them to the airport. Corporal, you stay with her and continue to provide first aid."

"Yes, Sergeant Major."

Martinez stepped back and motioned for them to get going. The sergeant put it in gear and pulled away and Martinez sighed, looking at his corporal.

"Let's hope I didn't just get those two killed."

"I don't think you had any other choice, Sergeant Major."

"I could have gone instead."

"She's one woman. You're responsible for over twenty on foot."

Martinez grunted. "Yeah, well, we better start hoofing it if we're going to catch up. As soon as the locals discover what happened, they're going to be pouring troops into the area and our gamble is going to turn into a bloodbath."

Harris/Dawson Residence, Lake in the Pines Apartments

Fayetteville, North Carolina

Maggie Harris sighed as she stared at where her fiancé's kit would normally be stowed, gone yet again. She had seen him for two days in the past two weeks. It didn't upset her. She had known what she was getting into from the beginning. Unlike most of the wives or girlfriends who had no clue what their new loves did for a living until the relationship was serious enough for them to be read in, as Clancy's assistant she had known from day one that Dawson wasn't logistics, that it was just his cover. He was a Delta operator who could be called away at any moment and sent on a dangerous mission anywhere in the world.

She loved him like no other, and despite everything they had been through, she wanted to spend the rest of her life with him regardless of the challenges his career choice posed. They had been trying to get married now for far too long, one incident after another causing them to put off their plans. It was simply too difficult to coordinate a large wedding with people coming from across the country and the world to finally see one of Delta's greatest bachelors tie the knot.

She was beginning to think it would never happen.

The doorbell rang and she smiled. The ladies from the Unit, the Better Halves Club, as they called themselves, had all made plans to get together after the barbecue had been cut short by yet another unexpected deployment. She opened the door and smiled at Shirley Belme, and within minutes, the apartment was abuzz and she forgot her troubles.

Shirley sipped on her mimosa. "What's up with you today?"

Maggie stared at her blankly. "What do you mean?"

"Something's on your mind. Something's bothering you."

Maggie sighed, her troubles apparently not forgotten. "Sorry. I thought I had put it out of my mind, but I guess not."

"What's wrong?" asked Vanessa.

All the side conversations came to a halt as everyone focused on their host. Maggie batted a hand at all the attention. "Oh, it's nothing. Just a little depressed."

Shirley rubbed Maggie's arm. "What is it, dear?"

Maggie's shoulders slumped and her eyes burned. "It's just the wedding. I don't know when we're ever going to get to do it. We almost never have time to talk about it, and trying to coordinate with so many people when he's always getting called away, I just don't know what to do. Yes, he could take a week's vacation and be pulled out of the rotation, but he wants his entire team to be there and so do I. But you can't take an entire team out of the rotation like that. I just don't know what to do anymore. Maybe it's best we just call it off."

Angela eyed her. "You don't mean break it off with him?"

Maggie vehemently shook her head. "Oh, no, no, nothing like that. Just continue like we have been. I mean, we've been doing it for so long now, a piece of paper and a wedding band wouldn't really change much in the grand scheme of things, would it?"

"Only for the better," said Shirley. "There's nothing like being married to the man you love."

Maggie burst into tears and Shirley led her to the couch where they both sat. "I so want to be married to him. I can't imagine not being. We have to figure something out and I just don't know what that could be."

Vanessa perched on her coffee table. "I thought Atlas said BD gave you free rein for the wedding? He said whatever you want to do is fine by him."

Maggie sniffed. "He did."

Vanessa threw up her arms. "Then what's the problem? This is about you two, not everyone else. Who actually needs to be there to make this day special?"

"The Unit, of course, my immediate family, his immediate family, but just organizing that small of a wedding is a nightmare. It's not like you can get last-minute caterers and ministers."

"Forget all of that," said Vanessa, batting a hand. "I'll cater it. I just need two days' notice."

Shirley leaned forward. "And I'll talk to Colonel Clancy. I bet you he would love to officiate. Venue?"

"Behind the Unit?" suggested Jagger's wife.

Angela frowned. "Not very romantic."

"It depends on how you look at it. Maggie, where did you two meet?"

"At the Unit."

"Exactly. And where did the sparks first fly?"

"At a barbecue behind the Unit."

Jagger's wife folded her arms. "See, I think it's actually very romantic."

Maggie stared at her friends, their enthusiasm contagious. "Do you really think we could do that?"

"Absolutely, the only question is when?"

Maggie bit her lip. "That's the problem, isn't it? That's what the problem has always been. Setting a date."

Shirley smirked. "Then let's not set a date."

Maggie stared at her friend. "What do you mean?" Her eyes shot wide. "Oh, I get it." A smile spread. "That's perfect!" She jumped to her feet. "Okay, ladies, we have a wedding to plan!"

En route to the Yangon International Airport

Yangon, Myanmar

Marsha woke with a gasp and a pain in her chest more excruciating than anything she had ever experienced. Her eyes fluttered open and she was surprised to find Corporal Dell leaning over her, his hand pressed into her chest, her immediate thought that he was being a little fresh.

"What's going on?" She was shocked at how weak her voice was.

"You were shot."

Her panic, calmed while unconscious, shifted into high gear once again. She asked the only question that mattered. It didn't matter who shot her or why or how she ended up where she was. Only one thing mattered.

"Am I going to be all right?"

Dell didn't answer directly. "I just need you to stay calm. We're almost at the airport. We've already radioed in. We've got medics on the plane that will fix you right up, but you need to fight, you hear me? You fight like you've never fought before. You just stay calm and steady your breathing. Focus on me. Don't worry about anything else. Just focus on me."

She closed her eyes, tears rolling down the side of her face burning a path to her ears. She was dying and it was her fault. If she had been slim and healthy, she never would have been in the vehicle to get stopped at the roadblock. If she wasn't so prone to panic attacks, she might have remained calm instead of escalating things by getting out of the car and shouting at a man who could barely understand a word she said.

She opened her eyes. "Did I get anyone else killed?"

Dell smiled down at her. "Just the bad guys."

She closed her eyes. "Thank God." She was growing weaker. The end was near. She stared up at the young corporal and struggled to lift a hand to grab him by his fatigues, but she couldn't. Her shoulders slumped in resignation. "Tell Mommy and Daddy that I love them and that I wasn't in pain. Oh, God, please don't tell them I suffered."

Dell took her hand and squeezed it. "I'll personally deliver the message."

She closed her eyes, her body racked with sobs, sobs that only hastened her own demise. "I need one more favor."

"Anything."

"In your report, don't make me out to be too much of a screw-up."

He laughed and squeezed her hand. "My report will read that you bravely attempted to reason with the soldiers, who then shot you unprovoked."

But his answer went unheard as she drifted into nothingness, wondering where the bright light was she had always been told to expect.

CHARLIE FOXTROT

Why did I have to waste my life?

Adjacent to Sware Taw Myat Road

Yangon, Myanmar

Jennifer continued to push through the unfamiliar side streets of Yangon. Her upper thigh was on fire, the large shard of bamboo that had pierced her skin either wasn't her only injury or had torn something. She wasn't worried about dying or bleeding to death, but she was quite certain she had partially torn a muscle when she fell. A proper look from a medic and rest and relaxation was all she needed, but all of that lay at the end of this torturous journey.

A message had been whispered down the line from Sergeant Major Martinez that the convoy of vehicles had reached the airport. She was at the rear of the pack now, leaning heavily on a two-by-four someone had found, the corporal bringing up the rear encouraging her quietly until a few moments ago when he had fallen silent. Through her pain, she glanced over at him, expecting to find him simply focused on the task at hand, but instead found a somber expression.

"What's wrong?" she asked as she continued to hop forward.

He flinched and shook his head. "Nothing."

The answer was a little too rapid. "Something went wrong, didn't it? That gunfire?"

The corporal frowned. "One of the passengers was shot."

She gasped, a painful lump forming in her throat. "Who?"

"I can't remember her full name. Marsha something."

Jennifer cried out in shock, cutting off the outburst with a slap of a hand over her mouth. "Is she all right?" But she already knew the answer from his expression.

He shook his head. "She didn't make it."

Tears flowed freely now. She squeezed her eyes shut for a moment, picturing her friend and her boisterous laughter. She was a large woman, larger than life, but so much of what she projected to those around her was a mask that hid her physical and mental pain.

Your suffering is over my sweet, dear friend.

She opened her eyes and noticed she had fallen behind again. She had no doubt that would have been Marsha's fear tonight, and Jennifer was determined not to be the one who put anyone's life at risk. She clenched her teeth tight and pushed forward, picking up her pace, grunting through the pain, determined to be at the head of the pack when they arrived at the airport, rather than an anchor that had slowed them all, putting them at risk.

En route to Myanmar

Red woke and stretched in his cot, the C-5 Galaxy configured to give the team of twelve rack space so they could get as much sleep as possible before they landed. He could sleep pretty much anywhere on anything, though there was something that he found soothing about dozing on an aircraft like this with the constant drone of the engines and the rattling of everything that had any bit of play.

His phone vibrated with a message and he fished it out of one of his pockets, the device connected to the plane's Wi-Fi. It was from his wife.

Can you keep a secret?

I've been trained to keep secrets even under threat of torture.

A smiley face returned.

When you guys get back, BD and Maggie are getting married immediately. We just need to know when you'll be here.

His eyebrows shot up. The ladies of the Unit were up to something, obviously. His best friend's wedding plans were continually interrupted, as if someone was conspiring to keep Dawson and Maggie apart. He had

64

known Dawson for a long time, and Maggie was the only woman Dawson had ever loved. Red had always assumed his best friend would die a bachelor and was delighted when Maggie insinuated herself into Dawson's life, recognizing that he would never make the first move. If those two didn't get married soon, Red wasn't the only one who feared they might give up, not for lack of love, but fear of continually disappointing the other.

He fired back a reply.

Not sure when we'll be back. Watch the news.

A question mark came back and he smirked.

As soon as I know, you'll know.

Thank you.

Nap time. TTYL. Love you.

Love you too. Don't tell anyone else, especially Niner.

LOL! I won't.

He put the phone back in his pocket then rolled over onto his side, facing the fuselage, and fit his sleep mask back in place. He had no idea what the ladies were planning, but he couldn't wait to find out.

North of Pyay Road

Yangon, Myanmar

Sirens filled the streets around them and the tension level had ratcheted up severely among not only her compatriots, but their Marine escort as well. Whatever had happened at the incident that had killed Marsha was triggering a reaction from the military that ruled this country with an iron fist. Jennifer was about midway through the group now, having pushed past the pain, accepting that any suffering was better than the alternative and was finite—as soon as she was on that plane, her suffering would subside and eventually be forgotten, unlike poor Marsha, whose life was over, all because some idiot didn't follow protocol.

She admonished herself silently. She couldn't blame Louise. If the roles were reversed, she might have done the same, though she hoped she wouldn't. It was drummed into you from day one to never get out of your vehicle at the scene of an accident. If the vehicle could still drive, you drove, and you got your ass to the first safe haven then reported it. Accidents happened every day around the world and embassy staffers were bound to get into some. The diplomatic plates they used, however, far too often made them victims of scammers. It had become so bad in Russia that those who drove nicer cars began mounting dashboard cams so they would have proof that somebody had intentionally walked in front of their vehicle or faked being hit. The scam wasn't unique to Russia. It was worldwide, especially in poor countries where people were desperate enough to let themselves get injured, hoping for a big payout from a rich country.

But that was not what happened. No little girl was involved in the scam and no mother would endanger her child like that just for a chance at a payout. A little girl had run onto the road to get her ball without looking and had paid the ultimate price. That would have been the end of it if protocol had been followed. But now other locals were dead and so was Marsha, and she had no idea how bad things might get if they were caught attempting to escape, or weren't caught and successfully escaped.

Those left behind at the embassy might find themselves slaughtered by the mob, whipped up into a frenzy, told that the evil Americans had murdered eleven people, including a little girl, all to get out of a traffic accident.

It was infuriating.

Sickening.

It was a perfect example of what happened when there was no freedom of the press, where the only source of information was a corrupt regime. But it was a problem the world over, including back home where the press had become partisan, labeled as fake news not because it was necessarily fake, but because it was clearly biased. It forced people to seek alternatives, and unfortunately those alternatives were social media where the algorithms were specifically designed to expose people only to the truth the algorithms thought they wanted to hear. The result? A country tearing itself apart, where once reasonable people were now at each other's throats.

It was part of the reason she loved her job, and that wasn't a good thing. Loving your job because you loved your country was one thing. Loving it because it got you out of your country, was an entirely different thing. She just wished people could remember the old America, where everyone got along for the most part. You went out, you voted. If your side won, you rejoiced. If it didn't, you licked your wounds, accepted your loss, and planned for the next election. You didn't hate your neighbor, you didn't hate your family members for thinking differently politically. Sure, there were spirited debates, but it would rarely end in estrangement.

America had to get back to its old values. Both sides had to look at each other and realize that things couldn't continue like this. If America were to remain the beacon of hope and freedom that it had always been, the hate on both sides had to stop. Today, people were so on edge that just the mention of a single word was enough to trigger them into a rage, and it was especially sad when it was out of ignorance because their only source of information was people whose job was to stir the pot.

The group came to a halt and she took the opportunity to continue to the front, and she smiled at the sight ahead. Nothing but grass then the lights of the airport. They had almost made it, but so much could still go wrong.

Approaching Yangon, Myanmar

Major Curt "Stacker" Kroger adjusted his heading slightly as he guided the C-130J Hercules into hostile airspace. They were skimming the waves, coming in below the radar in the dead of night, which always made things a little more interesting. He wasn't concerned. They trained for this. It was what would be waiting for them at the airport that had the sweat trickling down his back.

They had been holding off the coast, waiting for the go-ahead received only minutes before—the group on foot had reached the fence line. This was when things could go seriously wrong. Everything hung on how the Myanmar military would react to his landing unannounced on their runway. His briefing indicated diplomatic negotiations had already been abandoned, the corrupt regime refusing to honor international treaties that allowed for an embassy to be evacuated unmolested.

"We're in Myanmar airspace," announced his copilot, Captain Chuck "Snowball" Evans.

"Acknowledged." He increased altitude slightly as he eased back on the throttle, preparing for a combat landing. His F/A-18E Super Hornet strike fighter escorts blasted past him, blazing a trail that would light up any surface-to-air missile sites in their path. Missiles streaked past him from the rear escorts, four explosions erupting ahead as radars activated by the lead escorts sealed the fate of those manning the weapons platforms.

"I guess they know we're coming now," muttered Evans.

"I guess so." He followed the river in as they left the coastline behind them, slowly increasing his altitude as more explosions lit the skyline ahead. Viper attack helicopters thundered past as he continued to reduce speed.

Evans pointed. "There's the airport."

"Copy that. Command, this is Rescue One. We have the airport in sight. Are we a go for evac, over?"

"Affirmative, Rescue One, you are a go for evac. I repeat, you are a go for evac, over."

"Roger that, Command, we are a go for evac. Beginning descent, over." He activated the internal comms so the personnel in the hold could hear him, putting on his best airline pilot voice. "Everyone, this is your captain speaking. We are about to land and the locals aren't happy. Make sure you're strapped in, because this is going to be the shittiest landing you've ever experienced. Good luck to us all."

Hoots were the response from the rear of the plane.

He exchanged a grin with Evans. "I think those bastards are looking forward to it."

Evans chuckled. "A lot of those guys have experienced carrier landings. Anything you do will feel like a hug compared to that."

Kroger grunted. "We'll see about that."

More explosions ahead followed by tracer fire from anti-aircraft positions ended any frivolity.

Myanmar wasn't giving up so easily.

Outside Yangon International Airport

Yangon, Myanmar

Jennifer hesitated, as did everyone, as Sergeant Major Martinez urged them through a hole cut in the fence surrounding the airport. Explosions rocked the city behind them and bullets streaked the air overhead. She was at the front of the group, and the sergeant major grabbed her by the arm as she stood frozen.

"Head for the end of the runway, now. Run as fast as you can. Don't stop for anything."

She snapped back to reality. The panic wasn't gone, but the indecision was. She stepped through the opening and made for the end of the runway where a cluster of people were already waiting that she recognized as those taken by car. Something thundered overhead and she glanced back to see the scariest helicopter she had ever witnessed in person race past her, bullets and missiles erupting from the shadowy machine, explosions ahead silencing the weapons firing from the other side of the airport.

As she spotted more choppers spread out to her left and right, taking out their own targets, people sprinted past her, some in silence, some screaming in terror. She grimaced with pain, hobbling forward as fast as she could when a rumbling sound grew louder by the second behind her. She didn't bother looking back. It didn't matter what it was. There was nothing she could do about it. Whether it was good or bad, she just had to reach that runway to be there when the plane arrived so no one would be waiting for her.

"There it is!" shouted someone.

She still didn't look, instead focusing all of her attention on the small group ahead that still seemed impossibly far. A large plane blasted overhead and she gasped as the shock hit her, the thunder of the propellers shaking her to her core. The force of the air almost knocked her off her feet and she was sure she would have been flat on her ass if she didn't have her two-by-four. Many of those around her stopped to gawk and she pushed forward, taking those precious seconds to make up some of the gap. The tires chirped as the plane hit the runway and she continued to hobble, the advantage she had gained by being at the head of the group now lost.

Somebody came up behind her. "Sorry, ma'am, no choice." Martinez stopped her then lifted her off her feet and hoisted her over his shoulder in a fireman's carry. She didn't bother protesting as she dropped her makeshift walking stick. If the sergeant major thought it was necessary to carry her the rest of the way, then it was necessary. She had tried her best and failed, though she had almost made it to the group. She closed her eyes rather than stare at the man's buttocks, and winced with every step he took, a fireman's carry effective but incredibly uncomfortable. "We're almost there, ma'am. You hang in there."

She smiled slightly at the gung-ho attitude. "Sergeant Major, I think I'm the one who's supposed to be encouraging you."

He laughed. "Don't worry, you're as light as a feather. I could carry two of you if I had to."

She flashed back to Marsha. This was why she had been put in the vehicles. There was no way she could have been carried like this, and there was no way she could have made the journey as quickly as they had to, especially this part.

"Here we go."

She was suddenly back on her feet and Martinez pointed at a corporal.

"Corporal, you make sure she gets on the plane."

"Yes, Sergeant Major."

She finally had a chance to take in what was going on around her. A large transport aircraft she believed the military called a Herc had just taxied to a stop, its rear ramp lowering. At least a dozen crewmen rushed out, one carrying a stretcher that for a moment she thought was for her when she saw them sprinting toward a nearby vehicle.

"Everybody on board, now! No hesitations, no delays. Just go, go, go!" shouted Martinez.

She moved forward, her agony forgotten momentarily as the rescue crew loaded the lifeless body of her dear friend on the stretcher then rushed back toward the plane. More gunfire erupted and she ducked on instinct. The corporal grabbed her by the arm, pulling her upright.

"Keep moving!"

She hobbled forward as fast as she could, then cursed and sprinted, no longer favoring her injured leg and instead screaming through the pain—there was no need to be quiet anymore. The plane was just ahead now, the ramp tantalizingly close. Tears flowed down her cheeks from the agony, from the terror, from the sorrow, and from relief as her foot hit the ramp.

She collapsed onto the hard metal floor and the corporal kneeled beside her.

"She needs medical attention!"

Two medics were immediately at her side. "What's the problem, ma'am?"

"My leg." She patted at the wound and they sprang into action as she laid down on the cool deck, her eyes closed, her chest heaving, the sounds of those around her filling her ears, panic and relief drowned out by the battle still raging outside.

The ramp closed and an announcement was made over the PA system warning everyone to strap in. The engines roared and they surged forward, the two medics draping themselves over her body to hold her in place. As the plane gained speed, another noise thundered over the familiar sounds of propellers pounding and engines whining, and they rushed forward even faster, lifting into the air as the plane shook with rapid thumping sounds followed by brilliant flashes visible through the portholes.

"Just chaff, ma'am, nothing to worry about," said one of the medics, sensing her fear.

"Prepare for hard-to-starboard roll," warned the pilot.

76

The two medics pressed harder against her and she wound her fingers through the grates on the floor as the plane suddenly banked hard to the right. She squeezed her eyes shut, picturing what was happening outside. The plane had been oriented toward the north and now they would be banking toward the south. The city was located near the mouth of a river not far from the coastline, and then all they needed to do was get twelve miles out and they would be in international airspace.

They leveled out, finally heading in the right direction, the engines continuing to roar as they gained speed. She steadied her breathing, distracting herself while doing the math. Certainly they were doing 100 miles per hour now. How far was it to the coast? Five miles? Ten? It had to be closer to five, then twelve miles to international airspace, make it twenty miles total. At 100 miles per hour, it was twelve minutes, but this plane was capable of far faster speeds than that, and in the next few minutes could be doing 200 or 300 miles per hour. Twelve would become six, would become three.

She settled on five minutes and began counting the seconds.

300, 299, 298…

But it had to have been at least two minutes by now. Could she safely remove 120 seconds?

177, 176…

The medics went back to work on her leg, distracting her. "How's the pain?"

She shrugged. "Better now that I'm not running."

"Do you want something for it?"

She shook her head. "Just give me a couple of Tylenol. I want to be completely alert."

"Good call."

Where was I? Maybe 150, 149....

"Ladies and gentlemen, we have just cleared Myanmar airspace and are in international waters. We're going to continue to push it for a few more minutes just to make certain we're outside of weapons range."

Cheers erupted and she smiled in relief, her head rolling to the side to see the others. But instead of smiling faces, she saw her beautiful friend Marsha zipped up into a body bag, and the guilt of surviving when her friend hadn't overwhelmed her, her smile replaced with tears.

Goodbye, my friend.

Operations Center 3, CIA Headquarters

Langley, Virginia

CIA Analyst Supervisor Chris Leroux leaned back in his chair at the heart of the state-of-the-art operations center located in one of the sublevels of CIA headquarters in Langley, Virginia. It was the end of a long shift in which a whole lot of nothing had happened. One of their operatives had spent the day in Pakistan waiting for the arrival of a target a local asset had assured them would be arriving at some time today, and they never had.

He hated wasted days.

This was the second time this asset had been wrong, and he was now officially burned. Sometimes an asset was wrong. It happened. Plans changed. People lied. But too often, some assets, desperate to make themselves appear valuable, would oversell a piece of intel. In this case, someone might have said that the target *might* be in the area today, but their asset had sold it as 'definitely would be,' hoping that he would be right and his value in the CIA's eyes would go up.

But that wasn't the case today nor was it the previous time. Now, they would merely take his intel and draw their own conclusions as to whether it was worth wasting resources on. In this case, one of their operations officers, Dylan Kane, had spent an uncomfortable day waiting for a target to arrive that never did, and Leroux's entire team had wasted not only their time, but the resources of an entire operations center, satellite assets, as well as support teams to get Kane in and now out.

Six figures wasted.

Sonya Tong, Leroux's second-in-command, tossed her headset on the desk. "Well, that was a waste of a day."

Randy Child, the team's tech wunderkind, spun in his chair, staring at the ceiling. "Maybe his car broke down."

Tong chuckled. "The dossier did say he was driving something British and notorious."

Leroux grinned. "That must be it."

Tong sighed. "In all seriousness, can we have Dylan shoot the asset? At least then the day might be worthwhile."

"Well, as much as I like the sound of that, something tells me the Chief wouldn't sanction the kill."

The door hissed open and their boss, National Clandestine Service Chief Leif Morrison rushed in.

"Speak of the devil," said Child.

Morrison eyed him. "I've been called worse by better."

Marc Therrien snorted from the back of the room. "Burn!"

Child's cheeks flushed as he dropped his foot to the floor, killing his spin. "Sorry, sir."

Morrison laughed as he joined Leroux. "Just messing with you, kid. But my ears are burning. I take it I was a topic of conversation?"

Leroux laughed. "Only in that you wouldn't give us authorization to eliminate our new source in Pakistan."

Morrison cursed, glancing at the displays. "Are you telling me his intel didn't work out again?"

"The target never showed."

Morrison cursed. "Burn him."

"Already done, sir."

"Good." Morrison turned to Tong. "Check and see if we've got a bird over the US Embassy in Myanmar."

"Yes, sir." Tong worked her keyboard and moments later a new feed appeared.

"Trouble?" asked Leroux.

Morrison gestured toward the screen as Tong zoomed in on the embassy, answering the question. "You tell me."

"Holy shit!" exclaimed Child from behind them. "What's got the locals so riled up?"

Thousands, if not tens of thousands, packed the streets surrounding the embassy, fists pumping in the air.

"Shades of Tehran, huh?"

Leroux shrugged at his boss. "A little before my time, sir."

"Watch Argo."

"Will do. So, what did piss them off? Usually the locals there, if they dare, are protesting their own government, not us."

"Apparently, yesterday, while en route to the embassy from the official residence, the vehicle carrying the ambassador's wife, driven by one of their Diplomatic Security drivers, hit and killed a little girl."

"Oh, no!" Tong gestured at the screen. "But that wouldn't really explain this, now, would it? Protocol says you don't stop. You head to the embassy and report the incident. How has it turned into this already?"

"A combination of factors," explained Morrison. "First, the ambassador's wife, Louise Chambers, didn't follow protocol. She got out of the vehicle to help the little girl. This sparked a reaction from the crowd and apparently the child's father charged her with a machete. The DS officer, Devon Crane, was forced to open fire to protect her, and as a result, the father was killed as well. The crowd that had gathered attacked them. He managed to get Mrs. Chambers back into the vehicle and was severely wounded in his own attempt to get back in. They managed to escape the scene but were pursued by multiple vehicles, and according to Mrs. Chambers, Crane realized he wouldn't be able to get them to the embassy before passing out, so he sacrificed himself by jumping out of the vehicle. She took control and made it to the embassy unharmed."

"And Crane?"

"Dead. They hacked him to pieces, quite literally. The local authorities moved in and recovered the body, or what was left of it, and have already turned it over to embassy personnel."

"How horrible," murmured Tong, wiping a knuckle across the corner of her eyes. She gestured again at the screen. "But why is this happening?"

"The military government is taking full advantage of the situation. They're claiming that Mrs. Chambers was driving, not Crane, that they both shot their way out of the scene, killing eleven, and they're demanding she be handed over to face charges."

Leroux folded his arms. "They have to know she's got diplomatic immunity, regardless of whether she was driving."

"Oh, they know, but they're playing games. They're saying that since we insist on calling them Burma, her diplomatic immunity is only valid in Burma, and they're now Myanmar."

"You're kidding me."

"Hey, you've read some of the briefs on this country. Very little that comes out of that junta makes sense. The legalities are irrelevant. All that is, is the reality. The situation on the ground is tenuous at best. There are thousands surrounding the embassy protesting, and more keep arriving. They're being bused in by the government. At some point, somebody's going to attempt to climb that fence."

Leroux scratched his chin as he regarded the satellite feed. "Haven't all non-essential personnel been sent home already?"

"They have, though it's still quite active."

"So, what are we dealing with here?"

"The last count we have, including the ambassador and his wife, is thirty-nine plus four Marines."

"Just four?"

Morrison nodded. "Last night, under cover of darkness, the majority of the embassy staff escaped. They were able to reach the airport and evac on a Herc with attack helicopter and fighter escort from the USS Ronald Reagan carrier group."

Child raised a finger. "Umm, I hope this isn't a stupid question, but why didn't they all just go out at once?"

Morrison faced him. "Not a stupid question. Somebody had to stay behind to keep the lights on."

"Huh?"

"Walk in front of windows on the compound grounds, make it look like they were all still there. If everyone had left, they would've figured it out and stormed the grounds then started a search. Once they saw our people weren't there, they would have begun searching for them."

Leroux chewed his cheek. "They must be pissed."

"And then some."

"So, what's the plan to evac the rest?"

"Delta's being sent in to attempt a direct rescue at the embassy itself."

Leroux jutted his chin toward the display. "Doesn't Washington remember Tehran? Last time we sent Delta into something like this, it turned into a Charlie Foxtrot before they even reached the embassy."

"They do, which is why the president was leery to authorize the mission, but the ambassador is a family friend, and politically he can't leave so many American citizens twisting in the wind when he should have ordered the full evacuation of the embassy months ago. That's why we've been tasked to come up with options using our resources and bag of tricks that the Pentagon doesn't have access to, just in case something goes wrong."

"And if it does go wrong?"

"The mission becomes a CIA op, and your team has been specifically requested by the Delta unit to be Control."

Leroux smiled slightly. "Let me guess. Bravo Team?"

Morrison confirmed his suspicion. "Bravo Team."

"And when's this going down?"

"Just after midnight local. That's around thirteen-thirty our time. Start positioning resources, activating assets, and coming up with contingency plans. Think outside the box. If this thing goes south, we may need to act in a hurry." Morrison headed for the door. "Figure it out and brief me in four hours. Oh, and try to figure out some way for everyone to get some sleep before this thing goes down."

Leroux glanced at one of the digital clocks on the wall. "We'll all just hop in the DeLorean, sir."

Morrison gave him a look as he opened the door. "There was barely enough room in there for Marty and Einstein. Our lives are action adventure not sci-fi. Figure it out." He left the room and the door hissed closed.

Child's hand jutted in the air. "I'd like to volunteer."

Tong eyed him. "For what?"

"To be the first one to hit the sack."

Leroux gave him a look. "Sorry, buddy, but I need you to let me know what options we have with their power grid, cameras, communications. You know the drill."

Child sighed and spun in his chair. "This is what I get for being so good at my job."

The entire room groaned in response, a round of fingers thrust in the air at him. He gave them a toothy grin as he continued to spin. "I love you too."

Leroux checked his watch. "Okay, we only have four hours before I have to brief the Chief. Contrary to unpopular misconceptions"—he looked askance at Child—"you're *all* critical. Everyone's on this exercise, and as soon as we have the contingency plans ready, then we all get rack time." He smacked his hands together. "Now, let's get to work and pray everything we're about to do is unnecessary."

En route to Myanmar

"The good news is they got the bulk of the staff out. Bad news is they lost one civilian and they have severely pissed off the locals."

Niner waved his tablet. "The briefing notes didn't indicate that kind of air defense capabilities."

"No, they didn't," agreed Dawson. "CIA says they had some reports of some stuff moved in through the black market by way of the North Koreans. The weapons systems were pretty primitive, so our guys were able to deal with it with little problem. But what it means is things were a lot uglier than expected. The Burmese took a lot more casualties than we had planned because of it. The hope had been to go in, land, get the people, fly out with nobody getting hurt. But at least a dozen positions were taken out. The Pentagon estimates as many as fifty dead."

"So, what does that mean for us?" asked Red.

"It likely means we're going in hot. We'll head in with two Black Hawks as planned with Viper attack helicopters and F-18s flying escort. The route we're taking in is the same one our boys did last night, so hopefully they've cleared the path. If they have, we get in, get our people, then get out, probably having to deal with small arms fire, but hopefully little else."

"And if they didn't clear the path?"

"We abort and figure something else out."

Atlas frowned. "Something tells me we've got only one shot at this. If we abort, those people are screwed. It's too bad they didn't get everyone out last night."

"Unfortunately, they needed decoys, otherwise what they did accomplish would've failed. Any questions?"

Red raised a finger. "Um, do you own a tux?"

"What?"

"Nothing." Red gestured at the parachutes. "I take it the Pentagon still didn't come up with the money to pay for tickets that included landing?"

Dawson chuckled. "No. Apparently, we're still on a tight budget, so they're just kicking us out the back end of this tin can. We'll be recovered in the water. It's the only way we're going to be able to insert tonight. There's no way we can delay this until tomorrow, and we definitely don't want to be doing it during the light of day."

Niner leaned forward. "Are you done?"

"For now."

Niner turned to Red. "If you need a tux, I've got one."

Atlas rolled his eyes. "If the man needs a tux, a boy's large isn't going to do the job."

Snickers filled the hold and Niner groaned. "I kind of walked into that one, didn't I?"

Atlas shook his head. "No. You ran full tilt into it." He turned to Red. "So, why did you ask about a tux?"

Red shrugged. "I figured they'd be pinning a medal on us for this."

"Wouldn't that need a dress uniform?"

Red shrugged again. "You're right. I don't know what I was thinking."

Dawson eyed his friend for a moment. Something was up. He could tell by Red's slight smirk, but what that was, he had no clue. He couldn't remember the last time he had worn a tux. Atlas was right. Any formal event he went to, he was in uniform unless he was guarding some VIP and had to blend.

Spock held up his tablet. "Have you seen these reports coming out of the embassy? Aynslee Kai somehow got in there. They've started throwing stones over the walls, and the bastards who are supposed to be providing security aren't doing anything to stop it." He checked his watch. "If this continues to escalate, we might not be able to wait until it gets dark."

Spock handed him the tablet and Dawson watched the report, the footage taken from the roof of the embassy showing a crowd even larger than yesterday's, and far angrier. Spock might be right. And if the decision to go in daylight was made, this mission might be doomed before it began.

Embassy of the United States of America

Yangon, Myanmar

Louise Chambers lay on the couch in her husband's office, exhausted. She was all cried out. She had nothing left. This was all her fault. So many people were dead, including Marsha, one of the dearest women she had ever met. She had played her part last night, walking in front of windows, turning lights on and off, walking across the courtyard, as they all had. When the missiles and gunfire streaked over the city, there had been panic, not only from within the walls of the compound, but outside, the crowd screaming in terror and running away from what they all assumed was the ultimate target.

A few stray bullets had pockmarked the walls, but no one had been hurt. The rescue operation had gone far more violently than they had been told to expect. The moment word was received that they had successfully made their escape, everyone except the four remaining Marines went to sleep, though she wasn't sure anyone actually managed to get any, at least nothing restful.

She stared at the television that had been playing all night, the volume barely audible, set to CNN International where Aynslee Kai continued to give regular updates on the situation to the world and to those back home. She could only imagine how worried her children were. She had managed to talk to each of them for a few minutes last night. She could hear the worry in their voices, and her heart ached, though not from their fear, but from the awkwardness.

Everyone knew it was her fault. She had broken protocol in a lapse of judgment. She had acted from the heart instead of the head. And when this was all over, she had no doubt there would be repercussions, not only for her, but for her husband's career. They were finished in the diplomatic corps, and any ambitions he might have had of going into politics were over.

The TV abruptly shut off as did the lamp on her husband's desk. She sat up, rubbing her eyes, noticing the drone of the air conditioning had stopped as well. The office door flew open and her husband rushed in. He grabbed the phone receiver and pressed it to his ear before cursing.

"What's going on?"

He slammed the phone down. "They've cut the power and our phones."

She stood. "But we still have the satellite communications, don't we? And the generators?"

"Yes, but the sat comms require power and the generators require diesel, and that's been hard to come by of late. Last week's top-up was only half of what it should have been, and yesterday's scheduled delivery never showed because of what's going on. We chewed through most of what we had just from the regular blackouts."

"What does that mean?"

"It means we can keep the essentials going for the next four to six hours and then we've got nothing."

She pulled at her shirt, already noticing the immediate increase in temperature. "It's going to get pretty uncomfortable in here."

"No shit." He sighed and extended his arms. She hugged him and he kissed the top of her head. "How are you doing?"

She shrugged. "I'll be fine. Don't worry about me."

He tilted her head back and stared into her eyes. "Hey, you're my wife and my best friend. It's my job to worry."

Her eyes flooded with tears she didn't know she still had. "You've got enough to worry about. But when we're back home, I'm demanding a week with you on a beach somewhere."

He pursed his lips. "Sounds hot."

She smiled. "I can take the heat, it's the ten thousand people that want to kill me that I'm troubled with."

He laughed, tossing his head back. He gave her a kiss then broke the hug. "I have to go update Washington on the situation. See if this affects their evacuation plan."

She tensed. "Wait, you mean they might move it up?"

"It depends. This is an escalation, and it could be a prelude to them storming the embassy. There's no way to really know. My guess is it's purely an intimidation tactic. There's no way they're going to violate the grounds. I'll see what Washington thinks."

She frowned. "I don't think it's the government taking over the embassy that we have to worry about. It's the pawns they've stirred up that are the real danger. If they decide to climb those walls, they'll tear us to pieces."

Her husband took her hand and kissed it. "I want you to stay by my side from now on just in case something like that does happen. I have a contingency plan."

Her eyes narrowed. "A contingency plan?"

He moved his suit jacket aside, revealing a shoulder holster and a handgun.

"Since when do you carry a gun?"

"Since ten thousand people decided they wanted to kill my wife and me."

"You're going to fight all those people off with one gun?"

He squeezed her hand, his eyes glistening as he stared at her, the pain evident. "The bullets aren't for them. They're for us."

In the Drink

Carrier Strike Group 5

Bay of Bengal

Dawson rolled over the side of the Zodiac. He loved skydiving but preferred to land on dry ground instead of water. The waves were a little choppy, but the Navy boys were doing their jobs well, half a dozen small vessels whipping around the area, recovering his team and their equipment. He was helped to a seated position by one of the crew.

"You guys are nuts, you know that?"

"That's why they pay us the big bucks."

"Well, the big bucks didn't really give you the big brains, now, did it? You joined the Army, but just jumped out of an Air Force transport to get onto a Navy ship. You should consider remustering."

"What, and miss out on all the fun? In the Army, I get to be all I can be on the land, sea, and in the air."

Niner dropped unceremoniously beside him. "Hey, BD. How the hell did you get in here before I did? You jumped last."

Dawson took his hand and hauled him upright. "Unlike you, I aim for the little dots on the water rather than try to avoid them. Less time swimming."

"Well, that's the difference between you and me. My aim's so good, I'd actually hit the damn boat."

Dawson gave him a look. "What? You're trying to say I'm a bad shot?"

Niner held up his hands in mock surrender. "Hey, I didn't say that. Don't put words in my mouth."

"Uh-huh. I think when this is all over, we're going to have a shooting match."

Niner grinned. "And what do I get when I win?"

"You get to live another day."

"Ooh, I always love it when the stakes are high."

"Don't be so confident. I'm not talking sniper rifles at the range. I'm talking the Close Quarter Battle Lane. Glocks and knives."

The entire boat rocked as Atlas rolled in. Niner grinned at him and Atlas groaned, turning to one of the crew. "Put me back in. I want to find another boat." They both extended a hand and helped the big man up, not granting his request.

"Just in time," said Niner. "You can be witness to our little bet."

Atlas' eyes narrowed. "Bet?"

Niner grinned. "Glocks and knives on the lane. Winner gets to live, or something like that."

Atlas rolled his eyes. "You two do realize that you both get perfect scores every time. You'll never settle whatever it is you're trying to settle on the lane."

Niner shrugged. "Oh well, I guess we both get to live another day."

Dawson's comms squawked in his ear and he raised a finger. "Control, Zero-One. Go ahead, over."

Clancy's voice responded. "Zero-One, this is Control Actual. The situation on the ground has changed. Prepare your team for immediate deployment, over."

Dawson cursed. "Copy that, Control. We're still in recovery. Should be able to deploy within the hour, over."

"Understood, Zero-One. Try to shave some minutes off that. Lives may depend on it."

"Will do, Control. Zero-One, out."

Niner looked at him. "What?"

"That was the colonel. The situation on the ground has changed. We're being deployed immediately."

Atlas shook his head as he stared up at the sky, the sun blazing down on them. "So much for the cover of darkness."

Niner sighed. "I've got a bad feeling about this."

Embassy of the United States of America

Yangon, Myanmar

"And we're clear."

Aynslee lowered her microphone. "How was that?"

"Perfect, as usual," replied Roy as he lowered the camera.

"Ha! You say that every time, even when I know I sounded like shit."

He shrugged. "What do I know? I'm a camera guy, not a sound guy."

"There's been a couple of times where I wish that were true. Me being accidentally on mute could have saved me a bit of embarrassment that time in Seoul." She gestured at the camera. "How are we for batteries?"

"We're good. I charged everything up overnight."

She patted the satellite phone in her pocket. "Yeah. I charged the phone last night too, just in case."

"I'm surprised they waited so long to cut the power. I would've thought they'd have done it as soon as they realized what was happening last night. I get the sense everybody's winging it, including our guys."

She disagreed. "I think the Burmese are certainly winging it, but that operation last night was well-coordinated. Military transport, helicopters, fighter jets."

Roy shrugged. "I suppose, but someone was killed. That might not have happened if they had used helicopters to come straight into the embassy."

"What do you think would have happened if they did that? They could have opened fire on the choppers and killed everybody, or the crowd might have stormed the place before they could get everybody out. There were a lot of people. That would have taken three or four helicopters at least, and from what I can see, there's only really room to land one at a time here, maybe two."

"So, you don't think last night was a cluster—?"

She held up a finger, cutting him off. "I think they prefer to refer to it as a Charlie Foxtrot."

Roy's eyes narrowed then widened. "Ah, clever. You learn something new every day."

She shrugged. "I prefer the original. Every time I hear it, I just picture Clint Eastwood in Heartbreak Ridge. 'It's a Charlie Foxtrot, sir.'" She frowned. "It doesn't have the same impact."

Roy chuckled. "No, I suppose it doesn't."

A rock smashed on the pavement only feet away and she spun from it, covering her head.

"Are you okay?"

She nodded. "Yeah, but somebody's got a good arm. Let's get some B-roll footage then get back inside. Somebody's liable to start throwing Molotov cocktails next."

Roy frowned at the thought. "I never thought I'd be in favor of prohibition."

En route to Yangon, Myanmar

Niner sat in the back of the UH-60 Black Hawk and adjusted his body armor, the squeeze on his chest a little too tight. They were going in ahead of schedule, things at the embassy apparently having escalated. Their briefing, delivered as they got changed from their wet insertion, reported that power and phone lines had been cut off, the embassy's fuel reserve for the generators was subpar, and the locals were now hurling projectiles over the fence along with their government-provided slogans.

This time a different approach was being taken. They were telling the Burmese they were coming ahead of time. He could understand the reasoning—there would be no hiding the fact they were there, and the enemy had to be assuming that Washington would make a play to get the remaining people out, so they would be ready for it. By warning them ahead of time that they were coming and why, it was hoped the Burmese would simply back off and let the extraction happen.

"This mission has Charlie Foxtrot written all over it," muttered Atlas beside him.

Niner agreed. "You have to go sometime."

Spock cocked an eyebrow. "Hey, people, what's with all this negativity? We've inserted into worse situations."

Sergeant Gerry "Jimmy Olsen" Hudson scratched his chin. "Yeah, but did we ever tell them we were coming? Do you think the Pentagon called up Iran and said, 'Yo, Ayatollah, we're sending in some troops to get our people. Please just sit back, relax, and enjoy the show?'"

Niner rolled his eyes. "That was a shit-show from the get-go. When missions get political, things go south."

"Aren't they all political?"

Niner shrugged. "I suppose, depending on what your definition of political is."

Dawson got off his comms and turned to the half of the team in his chopper, Red no doubt about to give a similar update to the other half of the team in the second Black Hawk. "The embassy just lost their generators, so now they're on batteries. Hopefully, they'll last long enough for us to complete the mission. There are four Marines still on site led by a gunny who has experience. He's coordinating things on the ground. Chopper One, that's us, will land on the embassy roof, where half the remaining staff will get on board including the ambassador and his wife. Chopper Two will land on the rear lawn and collect the rest. We depart immediately, returning the way we came in. From crossing into their airspace and getting back out should be no more than fifteen minutes. If the Burmese keep their powder dry, this should be nice and smooth."

Niner eyed him. "Do you really think they're going to just let us go in right under their noses and get our people without reacting?"

Dawson grinned. "Not for a second, which is why we've got half a dozen Vipers and eight F-18s coming along for the ride."

Jimmy frowned. "And if we get shot down?"

"Head south to the river, commandeer a boat, and sail it out to the ocean."

Atlas sat back. "So, in other words, don't let the locals take us?"

"Unless you want to have a really bad day."

Niner jammed his fists into his hips and thrust his chest out. "Never give up! Never surrender!"

Spock groaned. "You had to get him started."

Dawson wagged a finger. "I am *not* taking credit for that." He resumed the briefing. "The primary mission is to protect the embassy staff. This whole country wants to tear them apart. If the locals get their hands on them, they're as good as dead, and so are we for trying to get them out. I'm not saying to actively shoot civilians, but once you're on the ground, you'll each have to make that judgment call. ROEs allow us to defend ourselves against any and all hostiles."

Niner fell silent, as did the others. They had killed civilians in the past, though that was a classification that blurred heavily outside of the Western world. Far too often in the hell holes of Africa, the Middle East, or Asia, there were more civilian hostiles than there were uniformed. He never had a problem killing a man toting an AK-47 that wanted to kill him and his way of life, but this was different. These wouldn't be civilian terrorists who wanted to kill Americans because they were American.

These were people being lied to, driven berserk by their government for political reasons, thinking that a great injustice had happened and that America was using its military might to help its people evade justice.

He had seen the video of the protest. Half the people there were women and children. This wasn't 1979 Tehran. This was something entirely different. And while he prayed things went smoothly, his gut told him that today would be anything but easy.

Embassy of the United States of America Rooftop

Yangon, Myanmar

Louise stood in the stairwell with the others, her husband directly behind her, a comforting hand pressed gently into her back. The helicopters were coming any minute now. They had split into two groups. Her husband had wanted her to go with the second group on the lawn where it would be safer, but she had refused. She wanted to not only be with him, but as the cause of this, she wasn't taking the safer seat from someone entirely innocent.

If anyone else had to die, she wanted it to be her.

Marine Gunnery Sergeant Lee Daily stood by the doorway at the top of the stairs. He acknowledged something over his radio then turned to them. "Okay, this is it, people. When I say go, you get up these stairs, go through this door, then head immediately to your left and straight for the open door of the chopper. The crew will help you in. I don't care if you hear gunfire, explosions, anything, you just get in that chopper. The sooner we're all in, the sooner we lift off, the sooner we're safe. Understood?"

Heads bobbed all around and her husband responded for them all. "We understand, Gunny."

"Good. One more thing. Don't worry about the rotors chopping off your head. Unless you play in the NBA, you've got nothing to worry about. Just run full tilt for that chopper."

Her husband raised his hand. "I played a little college ball. Does that count?"

Scattered laughter broke the tension and Daily smiled. "I think you'll be safe, sir." He pointed at the CNN crew. "And don't be slowing things up taking video or I'll leave you behind. Got me?"

Aynslee Kai smiled slightly. "Got you, Gunny."

The building vibrated and everyone tensed up again. Daily peered out the door. "Here they come! Get ready!"

Louise closed her eyes, saying a silent prayer for all of them, and she felt selfish for doing so. Yes, she wanted everyone to be safe when this was all over because it was the decent thing, but she also wanted them to be safe so she had nothing further to feel guilty about. She would be tortured by what had already happened for the rest of her life.

Wasn't that enough?

Over Yangon, Myanmar

Dawson took a knee by the door as the massive Black Hawk thundered over the city below, just above the rooftops. They were moments away from the exfil, and as he surveyed the ground below, watching for any missile launches, he found himself wondering just why the hell Red had asked him if he owned a tux.

"Sixty seconds!" shouted the pilot.

Dawson turned to the others. "This is it. As soon as we're on the ground, we exit, secure the rooftop, and as soon as the staffers are on board, so are we. Provide suppression fire, but don't fire blindly. Take out specific targets or just make a lot of noise. I want to be down and up inside of two minutes. Understood?"

"Yes, Sergeant Major!" replied his team in unison.

"Ten seconds!"

Crewmembers opened the side doors and Dawson grabbed a handhold as he rose to his feet, his M4 ready for whatever might come. So far, there hadn't been a single shot fired at them, which amazingly suggested Washington's tactic of warning the Burmese they were coming had had the desired effect.

This might not turn into a disaster after all.

Operations Center 3, CIA Headquarters

Langley, Virginia

Leroux stood in the middle of the operations center watching the various feeds from the mission unfolding in Myanmar. He wasn't Control yet, and so far it was looking like he might not need to take over. The CIA was only getting involved if one or more of the helicopters got shot down and this turned into a ground operation where CIA resources unknown to the Pentagon might need to be brought into play to save the lives of those trapped.

The first helicopter touched down on the roof of the embassy. The Delta operators surged from both sides, their weapons raised, heading for the edges of the rooftop as a door burst open and a Marine stepped out followed by a stream of civilians racing toward the helicopter.

"Holy shit!" muttered Randy Child behind him. "This is actually going to work."

"Don't jinx it," chastised Marc Therrien from the back of the room.

The second chopper landed on the rear lawn, the rooftop action repeating itself, this time on grass.

The door to the ops center hissed open and Director Morrison rushed in. "Status?"

"Both choppers have landed," reported Leroux. "Civilians are boarding now. No hostile action reported so far."

"Huh. I never thought telling them we were coming would have worked," said Morrison as he joined Leroux at the center of the room.

"Neither did I, but after the shellacking they took last night, maybe they decided their expensive new hardware should be saved for a rainy day."

"Could be."

"Oh, that's not good."

Everyone turned to Tong as she pointed at the screen's bottom-left feed. Leroux redirected his attention and cursed. The crowds were flowing over the walls and Myanmar regulars were opening the gates.

"Here comes the liquor," warned Child. Half a dozen explosions flashed on the screen as Molotov cocktails, until this point held at bay, were finally brought into the mix. But Molotov cocktails and rioting crowds didn't concern Leroux—the choppers should be in the air before any of that posed a risk.

Someone behind him shouted. "RPG!"

Outside the Embassy of the United States of America

Yangon, Myanmar

Captain Champo smiled. He had been right. When he had received word about his brother and niece, his request to deploy his men to the embassy had been denied, but after last night's escape by most of those supposedly trapped at the embassy, scores of units had been called into the city to prevent the last few from getting away.

His unit had been assigned south of the airport but that was a waste. There was no way the Americans would use it again. They would be coming in with choppers, directly to the embassy. He had left Lieutenant Kan with ten men, more than enough to defend against an enemy that would never be coming, and took the rest of his unit and deployed them around the embassy and to the south with RPGs. Their orders were to take out the helicopters once they were loaded and airborne.

He wanted maximum casualties.

He didn't want to take out the helicopter before the civilians were on board—that would just delay things and possibly allow for negotiations to defuse the situation. He wanted blood. Payback. Suffering. He wanted those responsible for killing his family to be consumed by terror in those final few moments of life as they fell from the sky then burned in the wreckage.

The first chopper was already on the roof of the embassy, proving his suspicions. He could barely see the top of it from this angle, but that didn't matter. He'd have a clear shot when it lifted off.

His radio squawked and he held it to his ear. "Captain, we have a second chopper on the rear lawn, over."

"Do you have a shot?"

"Negative."

"Redeploy north along the lake. That should give you a good angle when they take off."

"Roger that."

He gripped the handle of the RPG held at his side. The Black Hawk helicopter had been on the roof for barely a minute and it wouldn't be long before it lifted off. The crowd roared in rage to his right and he smiled to see the gate swinging open, enraged citizens pouring through it and over the walls, permission granted the blood-thirsty to satisfy their lust.

An RPG streaked across the sky from his left, the distinctive whoosh startling the crowd, and he cursed.

Someone had disobeyed their orders.

Embassy of the United States of America Rooftop

Yangon, Myanmar

"Everybody down!" ordered Dawson as he spotted the exhaust plume of a Rocket-Propelled Grenade racing toward them. It had been a trap all along. The enemy had lured them in, let them land, and when they were most vulnerable, acted. The question was, was it a one-off, or was this coordinated? The RPG whooshed past him and he spun, following its path, wincing as it passed over the helicopter's rotors by mere feet. "Did anybody see where that came from?"

"Incoming!" shouted Niner from the opposite side of the roof.

"Everybody down!" ordered Dawson again. He turned to see the last of the civilians boarding the chopper, the gunny facing him.

"We're good to go!"

Dawson pointed in horror as the rocket from Niner's position slammed into the rotors, impacting one of the massive blades, the explosion compromising the strength of the metal. It dipped as its integrity failed, and before anyone could say or do anything, one of

America's brave warriors was sliced in half. Dawson cringed. "Control, Zero-One, we're taking rocket fire here. Chopper One is disabled. One Marine gunny dead. We need those enemy positions taken out, over."

"Negative, Zero-One. They're firing from within the crowd, over."

Dawson cursed as what he suspected was confirmed. The only way to stop the RPG fire would be for the Vipers to shoot into the crowds, and even then, these weren't coming from fixed positions. These were shoulder-launched. "Zero-Two, Zero-One, status?"

"Zero-One, Zero-Two, we're good to go. Should I hold for you?"

"Negative. Depart immediately. Take the route over the lake to the north." Another missile streaked overhead. "It's getting too hot here. It's only a matter of time before they get in position to take you out. Depart now."

"Roger that, departing now. Zero-Two, out."

Dawson pointed at Niner and Atlas. "Put some lead on that courtyard."

Atlas opened up as Niner repositioned. Dawson glanced over at Spock who was checking on the gunny and the widower gave a slight shake of his head. Unfortunately, it was better this way. If the gunny had somehow survived, it wouldn't be for long, and he would slow them down.

The rotors were powering down and Dawson turned to the surviving Marine. "Corporal, what's the quickest way to the lake?"

The young man stared at him blankly for a moment, his eyes wide, his mouth agape.

"Marine! What's the quickest way to the lake?"

The corporal flinched then pointed at the door. "Down the stairs to the ground floor, then it's a straight shot through the corridor to the rear."

Niner's M4 opened up, joining Atlas and Jimmy's suppression fire. Dawson pointed at the door. "Corporal, make sure the path is clear then position yourself to direct the civilians."

"Yes, Sergeant Major!" The corporal disappeared through the door as Dawson continued giving orders.

"Spock, as soon as those blades stop spinning, get everyone out of the chopper and down those stairs."

"Yes, Sergeant Major!"

Dawson repositioned and peered out over the ledge. The crowd that had surged into the courtyard had backed off slightly as his men fired in front of them. It wouldn't take long, however, for one of them to test their resolve and discover that those holding them at bay had no intention of killing unarmed civilians. He glanced over his shoulder to see Red's chopper heading out over the lake, and he breathed a sigh of relief as it continued unmolested.

Now it's time to save ourselves.

He activated his comms. "Control, Zero-One. Mission failure, I repeat, mission failure!"

Over Yangon, Myanmar

Red cursed as he watched out the side door at the chaos below. The helicopter slowly banked, the airframe vibrating as chaff deployed from the defensive pods. Four Viper attack helicopters positioned themselves as escorts, deploying their own countermeasures as they headed out over the city and banked south toward safety.

Sweets cursed. "We have to get back on the ground! They're going to be slaughtered!"

Red jerked his chin toward the terrified civilians. "Negative, Sergeant. Our responsibility is to these people. Once they're safe, rest assured, we're heading back in."

Sergeant Danny "Casey" Martin spat. "We're glorified bellhops now. Our job is done. We've got another job on the ground."

Red understood the sentiment. He even agreed with it, but they were wrong. Their job wasn't done. Anything could happen where they might be needed. Jagger opened his mouth to say something and Red put an end to it. "Stow it. You have your orders."

"Yes, Sergeant," echoed his team reluctantly. They leveled out and Red headed to the front of the utility tactical transport helicopter.

"ETA?" he asked the pilot.

"Five minutes."

"Holy shit!" exclaimed the copilot. Red's eyes bulged at the sight of half a dozen RPGs screaming toward them from directly ahead. Their enemy had clearly pre-positioned men all along the escape route, making evac impossible.

"Get us on the ground, now!" ordered Red.

"I don't think we've got much choice in it," replied the pilot as the chopper dipped sharply and banked left. Red caught sight of the Vipers swarming ahead, more chaff deploying, their cannons firing wildly ahead in an attempt to take out the incoming projectiles.

"Everybody hang on!" yelled Red as he turned around. "We're going down and we're going down hard. As soon as we hit the ground, Bravo Team exits the chopper on both sides and secures the immediate area. Civilians, await my order to evac the chopper then flight crew, you assist. Marines, the civvies are your responsibility. You shoot anything with a weapon that comes near them."

"Yes, Sergeant!" acknowledged all the military personnel.

"Brace for impact!" shouted the copilot. Red grabbed on to some cargo netting and widened his stance. An explosion erupted and the entire airframe was tossed, suggesting an impact from below. Alarms from the cockpit sounded and the crew leaped into action.

"New plan!" shouted Red over the din as they hurtled to the ground. "When we hit the ground, Bravo Team, secure the area. Everyone else get your ass out of the bird and clear." He pointed overhead. "And watch the rotors! They may be tilted!"

"Brace for impact!"

Moments later they slammed into the ground. Red let the bend in his knees absorb the impact then leaped into action. "Bravo Team, secure the area!" His men poured out both sides and he jumped out as well. He activated his comms as he swept his arc. "Control, Zero-Two, Chopper Two is down. I repeat, Chopper Two is down!" He glanced over his shoulder and back into the hold. "Is everyone all right in there?"

One of the Marines responded. "Yes, Sergeant, no injuries."

"Control, we are on the ground. No injuries. The bird is toast. I believe we are approximately two klicks southeast of the embassy. Can you confirm, over?"

A new voice came over his headset and he smiled. It was Chris Leroux, a man they had worked with on countless missions. His CIA team was second to none and had assets available to them that could do things anyone in the Pentagon would be brought up on charges for even thinking about. The CIA didn't operate under the same rules as the military, and it just might be what they needed to save their asses today. "Confirmed, Zero-Two. We have you two-point-five klicks, south-southeast of the embassy. We're showing enemy units moving in on your location from all directions. There's an alleyway just east of you, just to the left of the red canopy. Do you see it?"

Red glanced over his shoulder, spotting the canopy in question then the alley. "Affirmative, Control. I see it."

"Get in there. Follow it all the way to the end. We need to get you away from the crash site as quickly as possible."

"Roger that, Control. Stand by." Red turned to his team. "Sweets, Casey, clear that alleyway!"

Sweets and Casey rushed to execute their orders, disappearing down the narrow laneway, Sweets' voice coming in over the comms a moment later. "Zero-Two, Zero-Nine. The way is clear, over."

"Copy that, Zero-Nine." Red directed the group with rapid hand gestures. "Everybody down the alleyway, now!"

The Marines herded the civilians toward their escape route and the flight crew followed. The pilot hopped down from his chopper, a series of small explosions erupting behind him as the self-destruct mechanisms he had triggered kicked in, rendering the helicopter useless, all of its electronics, classified or otherwise, obliterated. Red urged them into the alley then followed Sergeant Trip "Mickey" McDonald and Jagger, covering their sixes.

"Zero-Two, Control. When you reach the end, hang an immediate right then go straight approximately fifty meters and take a left just ahead of the bright green apartment building, over."

"Roger that, Control. Status on the hostiles?"

"First element should be arriving at the crash site in thirty seconds."

"Status on Chopper One?"

"Zero-One has declared mission failure. They're evac'ing through the rear of the embassy. Don't worry about them, Zero-Two. We'll take care of you both."

Red shuffled his way past some of the slower civilians, reaching the end where Sweets and Casey were already leading the group down the road toward the green apartment building. And while he had his own team and civilians to worry about, no amount of reassurances from Langley would have him not being concerned about his friends.

If Dawson were killed before Maggie had a chance to marry him, Red would never forgive himself.

Embassy of the United States of America Rear Lawn

Yangon, Myanmar

Dawson rushed out the rear entrance of the embassy, his expert eye quickly assessing the situation. The mob hadn't reached the lawn yet, the majority still concentrated in the front courtyard, attempting to gain access to the main building.

"—which can only be described as disastrous."

He spun toward the voice, cursing when he spotted Aynslee Kai standing in front of her cameraman with her mic to her mouth.

"One Marine gunnery sergeant is dead in a manner too disturbing to describe on the air to our viewers. The rescue helicopter is irreparably damaged and the American Special Forces unit sent in to rescue these people now have to save themselves as well." She pressed her finger to her earpiece and he cursed. This was being transmitted, not just recorded.

Is that idiot live?

"Yes, Sandy. Right now, we're attempting to escape through—"

Dawson stepped swiftly over and batted the camera down. "Are you insane, lady? You're about to broadcast our escape plan!"

Aynslee glared at him. "We're not live. We're just recording a piece for later."

"And you trust that nobody who sees this is going to leak the story? You've got the inside scoop on the biggest story in the world right now, and you're telling me some producer back stateside isn't going to be tempted to put that on the air?" He spun toward the cameraman. "Shut it off."

The cameraman, to his credit, ignored the order and instead looked to his own commanding officer for instructions as to what to do. Aynslee nodded and the camera was turned off.

Dawson stabbed a finger at her. "Nothing gets transmitted."

"Have you ever heard of freedom of the press?"

"I have. And you want to know what my orders are?"

"What?"

"To rescue the *embassy* staff. No one said anything about a reporter and her cameraman. So, if you want to be part of this rescue, nothing gets transmitted. Otherwise, I'll leave your ass behind and you'll be recording your final moments when that mob reaches you."

"You wouldn't dare."

"Try me, lady." Dawson jogged after the others and activated his comms. "Control, Zero-One. Our news crew was just transmitting a report stateside. They claim it was just being recorded. You might want to get somebody to call in some favors to make sure they don't air anything until we're out of here. They could compromise the mission

J. ROBERT KENNEDY

and kill everyone, including myself, which would be really disappointing, over."

Leroux responded. "Copy that, Zero-One. Unbelievable. We'll see what we can do at this end. Whoever wrote the First Amendment obviously wasn't taking into account that a couple of centuries later there'd be satellite feeds. Zero-One, your ark is arriving and I don't remember the Bible mentioning anything about two reporters being let on board. I'm going to leave it up to you, over."

Dawson chuckled as he spotted the boat approaching the shore. "I'll take it under advisement, Control." He spotted the grinning pilot at the controls waving at them as if nothing were amiss. "Your asset has arrived. Status on secondary evac?"

"Choppers are inbound now. We should have you out of there soon."

"Copy that, Control. Zero-One, out." The boat pulled up to the rear dock and he smiled at the familiar CIA operative there to save their asses. "What's a nice guy like you doing in a place like this?"

Jack glanced over both shoulders. "Nice guy? No idea who you're talking about. Now, get on my damn boat so we can get the hell out of here."

122

Outside the Embassy of the United States of America
Yangon, Myanmar

"Captain, they're escaping on a boat!"

Captain Champo cursed, raising his radio to his lips. "Everyone redeploy around the lake. Take out that boat!" He tossed his spent RPG to the ground then sprinted toward the embassy front gate, shoving through the crowd that numbered in the thousands. There was no way he was reaching the murderous Americans in time, but he had to try. He fired his AK-47 in the air and the crowds turned. He yanked his red scarf tied around his neck, holding it up, and they parted. He sprinted forward, reaching the front doors of the embassy, the crowds hammering at them.

"Stand back!" he ordered.

Those at the door made a hole and he emptied his mag into the lock, shredding the mechanism and weakening the reinforced door enough for the crowd to finish the job. He stepped back and waved, and the crowd surged forward again, the door giving way. He climbed over those who had fallen to the ground from their efforts and rushed through the entranceway, followed by scores of those just as angry as he was that the Americans were escaping justice for what they had done.

He had no idea where he was going. All he knew was that he had to get through this building to the rear lawn. He continued pressing forward and found a long corridor heading in the direction he needed to go. He sprinted down the length of it, his hopes raised at the sight of sunlight shining through a glass panel in the door at the far end. He shoved it open and found himself facing the lake. He bolted across the lawn, spotting the only boat on the small lake big enough to carry the Americans, and cursed.

They were too far away.

His phone vibrated in his pocket and he pulled it out to see a message from his sister-in-law, Garma.

I'm at the embassy. The Americans have escaped!

He quickly replied.

Not all of them. Before this day is out, I swear American blood will be spilled. My brother and little Nilar will be avenged.

A string of emojis was the reply and he responded with a thumbs-up, never one to indulge in the graphical representation of emotions. Thumbs-up/thumbs-down, yes/no, all right/not all right. He had no problem with that, but hugs and kisses and whatnot were ridiculous.

He raised his radio. "Converge on the north of the lake. Anybody who has a shot, take it. One week's leave to whoever kills the first American!"

Inya Lake

Yangon, Myanmar

Jack, just Jack, had been enjoying a perfectly nice day until he'd been called in last minute as part of a contingency plan should things go wrong on a ballsy and stupid rescue attempt. Last night's operation had succeeded, the fact only one civilian was lost a miracle. But if he were planning the op, he would have had choppers landing at the embassy at the same time as the plane was arriving at the airport, and got everybody out in one surprise operation. But he wasn't a planner at the Pentagon, thank God. Sitting at a desk would be sheer torture, and his cute ass wasn't known for having any excess padding. He preferred to be on his feet, taking action rather than sitting back and watching it happen.

He regarded Dawson. "You know, you grunts ruined my vacation."

Dawson eyed him. "Vacation? Where the hell were you on vacation that you were able to get here so quickly? Bangladesh?"

Jack jabbed a finger at Dawson. "Hey, outside of the rainy season, it's beautiful there."

"I have no doubt."

"You have to learn to appreciate the simple life, like most of the world lives. It's quite enjoyable in some ways when you're not worried about where your next meal is coming from and know that you can leave it whenever you want. Your little situation interrupted the start of a perfectly nice decompression escape."

"I'm sorry. It's all my fault."

They both turned toward the woman's voice. Jack recognized her from his briefing package as the ambassador's wife, Louise Chambers. And she was right. It was her fault. He regarded her. "Ma'am, I've read the briefing package, and it's your fault because you let a moment of humanity interfere with what the textbook said. People are going to blame you, especially the press and those on the other side of the political spectrum from whatever you are. But don't let them ever make you feel guilty about having a heart. The Myanmar government's been looking for any excuse to make our country look bad, and they got the opportunity with you. If you had followed protocol, something else could have triggered this a week from now. This is a corrupt, desperate regime. Anything that happened after you passed through the embassy gates is on them, not you. Anything that happens from now on, you have no part in." He jerked a thumb over his shoulder at Dawson. "If anything goes wrong, they'll blame him."

She smiled weakly, her eyes flitting over to Dawson. "None of you are to blame for anything that might go wrong. You're all extremely brave, and I know I speak for all of us when I say we appreciate everything you're doing for us."

Ambassador Chambers stepped forward, putting an arm around his wife's shoulders as Jack continued to guide them northward on the small lake. "What's the plan?"

Dawson glanced over at the reporter and her cameraman, filming everything being said. Aynslee held up both hands. "Don't worry, we're just recording. We're not transmitting anything."

Jack grunted. "You'd better not be. Otherwise, I'll be the first to shoot you."

Her eyes shot wide. "How dare you threaten me like that?"

Jack shrugged. "I eliminate all threats. So, if you become a threat to this operation, you're off the boat. And if I catch you transmitting, I *will* shoot you."

"I want your name."

Everyone on the Delta team chuckled.

"It's Jack."

"Jack what?"

"Just Jack," echoed all six Bravo team members, laughter erupting.

"I fail to see what's so funny."

Niner grinned at her. "Darling, I don't even know if this man's own mother knows his last name. And considering what business he's in, I wouldn't even count on Jack being his real first name."

Spock, his M4 aimed at the shoreline as he watched for hostiles, glanced over his shoulder at Aynslee. "And he's probably the only one on this boat that can kill you and not face any consequences."

Her jaw slackened slightly and she stared at Jack. "Who are you?"

"I'm Jack."

"No, I mean, *what* are you?"

"At the moment, I'm the ferryman taking you across the River Styx, and you following my simple rule of not compromising this mission is your payment in lieu of the coins you owe me."

Chambers cleared his throat. "Nobody's answered my question. What is the plan?"

Dawson responded. "We're all getting off at the north end of the lake, then it's a straight shot east where you'll be extracted."

"You haven't had too much success with helicopters so far, young man."

Jack smirked, wondering how long it had been since Dawson had been called young man on the battlefield.

"Everything's a distraction to the south. This particular extraction is coming from an entirely different direction that they won't be expecting. Don't worry, Ambassador, we'll get you and your people out of here."

They bumped up against the dock and the tour boat operator Jack had rented it from rushed over to tie it off. His eyes bulged. "You lied to me!"

Jack hopped onto the dock as the others disembarked. "Zeyar, my friend, I didn't lie, I merely omitted the entire truth."

"You'll get me in big trouble."

Jack drew his Glock and aimed it directly at Zeyar's chest. "Raise your hands."

Zeyar's hands shot into the air.

"Good. Now, if anybody sees us, you can tell them that you had no choice. I threatened to shoot you if you didn't cooperate. Now, where's our transport?"

Zeyar gestured to the right with a single finger, the hand it belonged to still high above his head. Jack glanced over to see an open-air bus, colorfully painted.

"Everybody on the bus. Now."

Dawson's team herded the group toward the loudly decorated vehicle that had seen better days. Jack had pulled this plan together with only 24 hours' notice, and when it came to mass transportation, beggars couldn't be choosers. They had been damn lucky so far. The boat he had managed to rent was the only one big enough on the lake for the job, Zeyar only too happy to take the equivalent of a year's wages for an hour-long rental since the tourists he had been catering to had dried up—with the military regime taking back control, the hopes of the briefly democratic citizens for a brighter future were shattered.

Jack glanced over his shoulder and watched appreciatively as the stunning Aynslee Kai climbed into the rickety bus. He jerked his head at Zeyar. "Let's go. You're driving."

Zeyar's shoulders slumped, resigned to his fate. They hurried toward the bus and Zeyar climbed into the driver's seat and Jack stood behind him, the weapon pressed against his back in case anyone was still watching.

"Let's go. You know where."

The engine roared to life with a plume of thick toxic exhaust, then they jerked forward as Zeyar popped the clutch.

Jack activated his comms. "Control, this is Jackrabbit. We're en route to the secondary LZ. Send in Valkyrie, over."

"Copy that, Jackrabbit. Valkyrie en route. ETA five minutes, over."

Jack turned back to the others. "Five minutes, people. Be ready to run like you've never run before."

Over Yangon, Myanmar

An explosion rocked Red's group from overhead as chaff deployed by a Viper attack helicopter successfully confused an incoming RPG. The F-18s continued to roar overhead, although they were useless beyond maintaining air superiority. The Myanmar military couldn't deploy any planes or helicopters to search for them, but the F-18s couldn't successfully target anything on the ground in their immediate vicinity due to the dense civilian population. The Vipers were sitting ducks from the RPGs as there was no radar system to lock onto.

The pilots valiantly held their positions overhead in an attempt to provide cover for his men and those they were here to rescue. They had managed to put about half a klick between them and the crash site, continuing to zigzag to the southeast toward the river, but there were simply too many civilians, hundreds, if not thousands, having spotted them.

And all it took was one to report their position.

Langley had so far managed to keep them from encountering any hostiles, but their luck would run out soon.

Leroux came in over Red's earpiece. "Viper Two, we've got a technical at your three o'clock heading north toward our people. Can you take it out, over?"

"Stand by, Control."

Red glanced up to see a Viper bank hard to the right then a missile launch. An explosion erupted just out of sight on the next street over.

"Control, Viper Two, enemy neutralized, over."

Red reached the next corner and peered out. Civilians were fleeing the area and just to his right, a jeep with a .50 cal mounted in the back was engulfed in flames. "Control, Zero-Two. Where are we headed, over?"

"Zero-Two, Control. Head right past the burning vehicle and continue forward until I tell you, over."

"Roger that, Control." He turned to the others and indicated with hand signals for them to advance.

Mickey joined him. "What do you think?"

Red grunted. "Let's just say Control's starting to sound a lot less confident."

"That's exactly what I was thinking. It's too densely populated. We can't get proper cover here. Those Vipers are going to have to bug out at some point, otherwise we're going to start losing more choppers. We need a less densely populated area that we can defend and our air cover can open up on."

Red advanced, covering the rear of their ragtag group. "No, we need to keep moving. We have to get to the river. It's our only hope."

Gunfire rang out ahead and a woman screamed as Sweets and Jagger's M4s opened up on an unseen target. Red rushed forward as Leroux calmly though urgently reported a rooftop sniper ahead. It meant ground troops were in position, and this just became a whole lot more difficult, if not impossible.

Operations Center 3, CIA Headquarters

Langley, Virginia

Leroux's eyes darted around the massive displays arcing across the front of the room. The operations center was abuzz, extra personnel brought in to assist with the major operation he had temporarily taken over with Dawson's pronouncement of mission failure. Both Black Hawks were down, with one Marine dead. It was a miracle that no one else had been injured or killed, but there was plenty of time for that.

Dawson's group was closing in on the secondary LZ where two Bell UH-1Y Venom "Super Hueys" were inbound that presented smaller targets and were more maneuverable. F-18s had just swept the area, taking out any radar positions, and Viper attack helicopters were providing escort. The screen showed all their assets in play, and he watched the choppers rapidly approaching a pulsing red zone. A cluster of blue dots, the Bravo Team members on the tour bus, slowly closed in on the same area. The timing had to be perfect, and for the moment, it appeared it just might be.

His concern was Red's group. The extra manpower was identifying military assets, whether they were vehicles or men on the ground, and tagging them in the computer, sophisticated software then tracking those targets in real-time on the satellite feeds. Hundreds were pouring into the area, quickly cutting off any means of escape. How the hell they were getting them out of there, he had no idea.

It was time to cause a little pain.

He turned to Child. "Take it down."

"Taking it down." Child tapped a single key on his keyboard, the order anticipated, the scripts he had written already tested. A secondary display in the bottom right showed the electrical grid status for the city switching from greens and yellows to reds. Another display just above it indicating the status of the communications networks, including cellular and landlines, cascaded into red as well. "That should wreak a little havoc."

Leroux hoped their young wunderkind was right. There was no hiding Red's team from the populace. There were simply too many people in the crowded city. What they needed to do was slow any response from the Myanmar military. Having people flood into the streets because their power was out, and kill the traffic lights and their ability to use cellphones and landlines to coordinate, just might buy them precious minutes.

This contingency was supposed to occur at night when it would have the most effect. The mission, having been moved up by half a day, had turned into the disaster he had feared. They should have waited, taking the chance that the enemy wouldn't storm the embassy, but hindsight was always 20/20, and even with the benefit of it, there was no way to predict what would have happened if they had waited. It could have turned into a massacre regardless.

He studied the screen, searching for anything that might help Red's team, but could see nothing. Swarms of red dots, each one representing an enemy asset, weren't just flooding the area.

They had already flooded it.

The satellite image zoomed in on Red's team showed muzzle flashes from Bravo Team members. They were already engaged, and that gunfire, regardless of the status of the enemy communications capability, would draw everyone in their immediate vicinity. If something didn't change, it would be a blood bath.

"Control, Zero-Two, we need instructions now, over!"

Leroux sat at his workstation, desperate to find a solution, but remaining calm. Panic was what got people killed. "Zero-Two, Control. Continue in a southeast direction as best you can. I'm afraid at the moment there are no good routes available, over."

"Copy that, Control. I'd like to officially declare that this mission is a Charlie Foxtrot. Zero-Two, out."

They had been figuring out how to get from point A to point B, but now it was time to think outside of the box. Perhaps they needed to figure out how to get from point B to point A. They were attempting to get to the river, but maybe there was some solution that could be found by looking at how to get from the river to where they were. He brought up some footage, including archival, zipping through a video taken by a tourist as they sailed up the river two years ago. He stared at the shoreline, watching for anything that could help.

Then he spotted it, and a smile spread.

Now to see how far we can get from point B to point A.

Kan Yeik Thar Street

Yangon, Myanmar

Zeyar barreled through the streets, hammering on the horn, repeatedly screaming at the top of his lungs with his head hung out the window in terror, as Jack's foot pressed firmly on the poor man's foot, shoving the accelerator to the floor. Acrid black diesel fumes belched out of the exhaust of the protesting bus as everyone hung on for dear life.

Dawson's team had all taken a knee in the center aisle, ducking low so as not to be easily spotted. The civilians they were responsible for, as well as Aynslee Kai and her cameraman, were sitting one per seat, attempting to hide their terror, but failing miserably, the erratic driving not helping.

Niner was directly ahead of Dawson, his hands wrapped around Atlas' waist, the big man gripping the seats on either side of him.

"What the hell are you doing?" asked Atlas.

"Holding on to the biggest paperweight I could find."

"The bus is heavier than me, asshole. Let go of me or I'm going to tear off that little pecker I'm feeling against my backside."

"That's my Glock."

"Bullshit."

"Well, I would say it's my M4, but you'd never believe me. I'm not a real man like you, Snuffaluffagus."

Snickers were heard, even from a couple of the civilians. Ambassador Chambers looked down at Dawson. "Are those two for real?"

"It never gets more real than those two, sir."

"I wonder what they would've done in the 'don't ask, don't tell' days."

Both Niner's and Atlas' heads whipped toward the Ambassador. "We both have girlfriends," they echoed.

Dawson had a little fun with them. "The policy might be gone, sir, but the closet's still there."

Niner let go, scrambling back a couple of paces, grabbing the handholds on the seats like everyone else. "I don't know what the hell you're talking about. I'm not in any closet. There's no room for me in my closet. Have you seen my closet?"

Spock cocked an eyebrow. "You mean the one that's filled with your pretty shoes?"

Laughter erupted from everyone as the exaggerated comedy routine put on by Atlas and Niner eased the tension of everyone, especially the civilians, who for a moment forgot their troubles.

The bus slowed with a jerk as Jack turned around, his foot no longer on the accelerator. "We're here, ladies and gents." He pointed ahead. "Two choppers, much smaller than last time. They make smaller targets and they're more maneuverable. They're going to have a hell of a lot harder time trying to hit those than those huge-ass Black Hawks with too much junk in the trunk."

Dawson rose and peered ahead, seeing the two Super Hueys landing with a bounce. "Bravo Team, escort the civilians to the chopper on the left. As soon as they're on board, the rest of us get on the second chopper. Marine and flight crew, you go with the civilians." He turned to Aynslee. "You two will have to come with us. There's not enough room on board that chopper for you."

"That's fine, Sergeant Major, we're sticking with you regardless."

"Why's that?"

Aynslee smirked. "Because I have a feeling you're where the story's going to be."

He jutted his chin toward Jack. "Same deal as he made with you. If I think you're going to get me killed, you go first."

She smiled. "It's a deal."

The bus jerked to a halt and Jack stepped outside. "Let's go, let's go, let's go!"

The Delta team hustled the civilians off the transport and the moment Dawson's boot cleared, Jack hopped back aboard as Zeyar slammed the bus back in gear and roared away. They sprinted across the field toward the choppers as Dawson and Spock hung back, covering their sixes.

Gunfire erupted to their left.

They had been found.

Lieutenant Kan leaped from the jeep and sprinted toward the park. Captain Champo had ordered them to redeploy from the airport once it became clear what the Americans were up to. Kan was monitoring two channels, one reserved for the Red Scarves, the other for the overall mission—he was receiving his discreet orders from Champo, but was also privy to what was going on overall.

Both choppers the Americans had sent in were down, one on the roof of the embassy, the other in the streets just southeast of it. But the Americans trapped at the embassy had escaped by boat then on a tour bus that had just arrived at the park located east of Kabar Aye Pagoda Road, where he had spotted two smaller choppers landing. He fired his weapon in the air to part the crowd, then rushed through, cursing at the sight before him. A group of civilians were boarding one of the choppers guarded by American Special Forces.

He roared in rage and raised his weapon, racing forward, determined to halt their escape. Two men spun toward him and gunfire erupted. Faint thuds shook his body, followed by blistering pain, and he collapsed, his weapon hitting the grass a moment before he did. Smoke popped, obscuring the escape as he gripped his unprotected stomach—there was no need for body armor while wearing a red scarf.

No one ever dared challenge them.

Until today.

Dawson and Spock both dropped to a knee, taking aim at a soldier running toward them. Dawson fired, taking the man out, then rose, falling back toward the helicopters as Vipers thundered overhead. He pulled a smoke grenade off his belt and yanked the pin, tossing it toward the gathering crowd. Spock did the same and they continued toward the choppers as more gunfire chattered, the sound suggesting the enemy was several streets over, firing at the helicopters overhead.

"All clear!" reported Niner, and Dawson glanced over his shoulder to see the first helicopter lifting off.

"Everybody on the second chopper!" he ordered as he and Spock continued to cover the escape.

"We've got you covered!" shouted Atlas, and both Dawson and Spock turned around, sprinting toward the helicopter as Atlas and Niner covered them. They leaped on board and the chopper strained to get off the ground, the plan never meant to include two reporters from CNN and their excess body weight.

Niner leaned toward the cockpit. "I can kick the big man out if you need to shed some weight."

"Let's just see what happens in the next ten seconds, or I might have to take you up on that offer."

Atlas rumbled. "I'll frisbee your little ass out of here before I'm going out."

They lifted off and soon were gaining altitude as they headed north. The Vipers fell into position, chaff deploying from all the airframes. The pilot glanced over his shoulder at them. "Looks like we're all going home today."

Atlas frowned. "Too bad, I was looking forward to seeing how far I could throw him."

Operations Center 3, CIA Headquarters

Langley, Virginia

Tong spun in her chair, smiling broadly at Leroux. "Both choppers have cleared the city limits."

Cheers erupted and Leroux decided Red's team could use some good news. "Zero-Two, Control. Just thought you'd like to know that Zero-One and his team have successfully cleared the city limits."

"Happy to hear that, Control, and I'd pop the champagne if I wasn't about to buy the farm. We're meeting heavy resistance. We need an exit plan and we needed it yesterday."

Tong looked at Leroux. "We have to give them something. These guys are goal oriented. Give them something at least remotely achievable and they'll do everything they can to get there. Right now, the river's just too far. They see it as hopeless."

She was right. Psychology played a factor here. Telling them they had to clear three miles of hostile territory on foot with no support was too demoralizing. He had spotted some sort of drainage pipe on the riverbank that appeared new or at least relatively new—the concrete surrounding the pipe was still solid. It led somewhere, the question was where? If he traced a direct line, it led to a new sewage treatment plant built five years ago. If Red's team could reach it, they could go through the pipe, bypassing over half a mile of the city streets.

But they were still two miles from there, and worse, he couldn't be positive the pipe and the plant were connected.

He sighed but activated the comms. "Zero-Two, Control. We have a destination. Approximately three klicks southeast of your position is a sewage treatment plant. That plant has pipes that run underneath the city and lead directly to the river. If you can get there, they won't be able to touch you."

"Control, did you say three klicks?"

"Confirmed, Zero-Two, three klicks. You think you can make it?"

"We'll make it or die trying. Zero-Two, out."

Leroux stared back at the displays as Dawson's two choppers did a wide arc around the city, the F-18s and Vipers taking out any military hardware that dared to engage. They would probably make it, though he wouldn't breathe easy until they were in international airspace and out of the range of any Myanmar-controlled weapons system.

He clasped his hands behind his head and frowned at Tong. "Two miles? Might as well be Twenty. We need to give them options. Otherwise, they *are* going to die trying."

En Route to Crash Site

Yangon, Myanmar

Captain Champo cursed at the report from one of his sergeants. Kan had been hit and was being taken to the nearest hospital, but wasn't expected to make it, another victim of these bastard Americans. Kan might only be his lieutenant, but he was also a friend. They had grown up together in the slums then joined the military and thrived. When they were off duty, they were equals, and now he had yet another person to mourn when this was all done.

The Americans had escaped to the north. There was nothing he could do about that now. That would be up to the air force, which, judging by the F-18s screaming overhead, it would be a job they would unlikely attempt.

But there was still the group in the downed chopper, and they weren't far from his position. The streets were jammed with people and his driver lay on the horn, attempting to clear a path. The only thing effective were frequent bursts from his assault rifle, but that wasted precious ammunition he intended to use on the Americans when he caught up to them.

"Captain, this is Shway," crackled his radio. "We've got eyes on the Americans!"

Champo smiled. "Where are you?"

"Just east of Dagon Tower."

"Take them out!"

"Engaging now."

Gunfire rattled and Champo fired in the air, clearing away the crowd a little more. "Get the hell out of the way!" he screamed. "I've got Americans to kill!"

East of Dagon Tower

Yangon, Myanmar

Red rushed past the crouching civilians, leaving Mickey and Jagger to cover their six. Sweets was on his knees, hunched over a woman lying on the ground as his team and the Marines fired disciplined rounds at an enemy Red had yet to spot, though he recognized an enemy .50 cal.

He glanced over his shoulder at Jagger. "Bring up the eighty!"

Jagger rushed forward with the Carl Gustaf recoilless rifle as Red reached Sweets' position. He glanced down at the civilian, the woman crying as Sweets dressed her arm. "Status?"

"She'll live. Through-and-through, nothing major hit." Sweets smiled down at her. "But it hurts like a bitch, doesn't it?"

"That's about the politest way I'd describe it," she said through clenched teeth.

Sweets tightened off the bandage as Jagger fired, a massive explosion erupting farther down the street, silencing the .50 cal.

Red rose. "Let's get the hell off this—"

He was cut off as two rounds slammed into his chest, knocking him off his feet. His head smacked the ground and his world went dark, his final thoughts surprisingly not of his family, but of the fact he wouldn't get to stand by his best friend when he got married in a few days.

En Route to USS Ronald Reagan

Andaman Sea

"Zero-Two is down! I repeat, Zero-Two is down!"

Bile filled Dawson's mouth at Sweets' report over the comms. The entire chopper fell silent as Dawson held up a hand. "Zero-Nine, Zero-One. Repeat your last, over."

"Zero-One, Zero-Nine. Zero-Two took two rounds to the chest. Checking on him now. Stand by."

Dawson stepped forward, poking his head between the pilot and copilot.

"Has the first chopper cleared international airspace yet?"

"Affirmative. They're clear and so are we."

"Then turn this bird around."

"I'm sorry, Sergeant Major, those aren't my orders."

Dawson pointed back at the city. "Those are my men fighting and dying, and they just lost their leader. They're outnumbered a hundred to one."

"We're a sitting duck in this," replied the pilot. "There's no way I can get you to their position."

"Then get us as close as you can. I don't give a shit if it's outside the city. We'll hoof it in if we have to."

The captain adjusted his mic and Dawson grabbed his shoulder.

"Sir, you know what they say. Better to ask for forgiveness later than permission now."

The captain cursed and they banked hard to port. "If I get court-martialed for this, I'm throwing you under the bus, Sergeant Major."

Dawson slapped him on the shoulder. "Just tell them I held a gun to your head. They'll believe it."

The captain laughed as he completed his 180 then pushed forward on the stick, bringing them toward the deck.

Dawson sat back down. "Zero-Nine, Zero-One. Any word, over?"

Jagger replied. "Zero-Eight here. Zero-Nine is working on him. So far unresponsive. He's not bleeding, but he took two direct hits to the chest and his heart stopped. We don't have a defibrillator, over."

"Do we have a defibrillator on board?" shouted Dawson.

The copilot pointed to a red pouch strapped to the fuselage. Dawson tore it off and the pilot glanced over his shoulder at him. "I don't know what you're thinking, Sergeant Major, but it's no use. There's no way I can get us in there. I'm afraid if your men on the ground can't figure out something…"

The pilot didn't finish his sentence. Everyone knew what it meant.

A friend, comrade, husband, and father, was dead.

And that wasn't acceptable.

CHARLIE FOXTROT

"Get as close as you're willing to go."

Operations Center 3, CIA Headquarters

Langley, Virginia

Leroux snapped his fingers. "Randy, get the power back up in that area. Sonya, find me the nearest defibrillator, hospital, clinic, anything close to their current position. Marc, bring up the protocols for using power from an AC outlet as a makeshift defibrillator. Joyce, contact the Ronald Reagan and have a defibrillator put on a drone for immediate deployment. Danny, find the nearest drone in the area that's rated to carry a portable defibrillator. Everybody else, keep doing what you're doing. Feed priority targets to the Viper and Super Hornet pilots. He's only got minutes."

Child's keyboard clicked away and Leroux glanced over to see the power system turning from red to orange as the tech reactivated the city's grid.

"Do you have that procedure?" asked Leroux, glancing back at Therrien.

Therrien frowned. "Negative. That's a bullshit movie trope. We need a real defibrillator."

Leroux cursed then glanced at the power indicators, now showing yellow in a couple of segments of the city. "Sonya, what have you got?"

"Nothing close enough. Everything's at least ten minutes away, and that's without being shot at."

Leroux activated his comms. "Zero-One, Control. We need a defibrillator at Zero-Two's position ASAP. Do you have one on board, over?"

"Affirmative, Control. We're heading toward his location now, however we don't think we can make it without risking all those aboard, over."

Leroux turned to Danny Packman, one of his senior analysts. "Drone?"

"I've got one over the target area. Where am I sending it?"

"Coordinate with the pilot of that chopper. Get them together on the ground ASAP."

"On it!"

"Zero-One, we've got a drone inbound. We're coordinating with your pilot now. Get some duct tape ready and tape the damned thing to the bottom of it if you have to. Seconds count, over."

"Copy that, Control. We're preparing to land now, over."

"Copy that. Zero-Nine, Control. We're sending in a drone with a defibrillator. Perform CPR until it gets there. There are no defibrillators locally within a useful distance, over."

"Copy that, Control," replied Sweets.

Leroux ran his fingers through his hair then grasped his skull, squeezing tight as the tactical display showed the drone and Dawson's helicopter both landing. Four figures jumped out of the chopper and sprinted toward the drone, and less than sixty seconds later it lifted off. He turned to Packman. "Status?"

"They're reporting successful attachment. Drone Operator is reporting successful lift off. ETA five minutes."

Leroux closed his eyes. Five minutes, plus the several that had already gone by. Was it too long? The book said if done properly, CPR could keep someone alive for over half an hour, and Sweets was trained.

It was in God's hands now.

"Zero-Nine, Control. Drone is inbound. ETA less than five minutes, over."

"Copy that, Control. Let me know when it's on the ground. I'll be busy here."

Tong pointed at the screen. "Um, did anybody notice that Dawson's chopper is still headed toward the city?"

Leroux peered at the overall tactical display and cursed. "Zero-One, Control. What do you think you're doing, over?"

"Control, Zero-One. We're joining this Charlie Foxtrot. We don't leave our men behind. Zero-One, out."

The finality with which the last word was delivered from Dawson suggested to Leroux that if he were to challenge the Delta operator's decision to head back into the fray, he just might find himself on the receiving end of a fistful of knuckles if they ever encountered each other again. Instead, he cursed and pointed at the screen.

"Find them a ride back to the city. Ideally something on the water. Let's see if we can get them closer through that drainage system. If he wants to get himself killed, let's see if we can at least make it difficult for him."

East of Dagon Tower

Yangon, Myanmar

"We can't hold them much longer!"

Sweets pointed to a nearby laneway that would continue their southeasterly route. "Take everyone through that alleyway. Continue southeast toward the sewage treatment plant."

"What about you?" asked Mickey.

Sweets grabbed Red and threw him over his shoulder. "We'll catch up, now go. That's an order."

"You heard the man!" Mickey opened up with his M4, providing suppression fire as the rest of the men, Marines, and flight crew led the civilians, including the wounded woman, across the street and into the alley.

Sweets spotted a flashing neon light for a restaurant not ten feet away. He rushed through the door, startled patrons and staff staring at him wide-eyed as they scattered out of his way. He lay Red on a table then removed his body armor and tore open his shirt. He checked again for a pulse but found none, and immediately began chest compressions, singing the Bee Gees' Stayin' Alive in his head to maintain the rhythm.

The gunfire outside continued to fade as the group he was now responsible for made their escape, and he prayed they made it now that they were down two guns.

"Where's that drone, Control?"

"Sixty seconds, Zero-Nine."

Sweets turned to those in the restaurant, cowering against the walls. "Does anybody speak English?"

Nobody said anything.

"Please, I need help here!"

A young man stepped forward. "I-I speak English."

"Good. Do you know CPR?"

The man shook his head.

"Fine." Sweets jerked his chin toward the street outside. "A drone is going to be landing there in the next few seconds. When the propellers stop moving, I need you to pick it up and bring it inside."

The man's eyes bulged. "I-I can't help you."

Sweets motioned at his M4. "If anyone asks, tell them I threatened to shoot you all if you didn't help. Understood?"

The man nodded as the high-pitched whine of the drone cut through the chaos outside.

"Get ready!"

The man rushed to the door, terror written on his face, then darted into the street as the drone set down, its propellers winding to a halt. A moment later the man reappeared with the drone in his hands, struggling with the heavy load.

"Just flip it upside down and get me that red package that's taped to the bottom."

The man complied and Sweets put his medical training to use, prepping the Automated External Defibrillator. He pressed the button and Red's body shook from the jolt, the machine reporting back that it had failed to detect a normal rhythm. Sweets closed his eyes and stared up at the heavens.

Please, God, if one thing goes right today…

The machine signaled another shock and Red gasped. Sweets checked the display and the confirmation of normal sinus rhythm and a weak but strengthening pulse, the O2 stats improving rapidly.

"Control, Zero-Nine. He's back!"

"Copy that, Zero-Nine. Once he's stable, let us know so we can guide you out, over."

"Roger that." Sweets smacked Red on the face. "Are you with us?"

Red stared up at him. "What the hell happened?"

"You were dead."

"Cool, and I'm not anymore?"

"I don't know. You tell me."

Red shrugged. "I don't feel dead."

"That's a start. Can you walk?"

"I don't know, but let's give it a try." Sweets hauled Red to his feet and the operator looked down at his bare chest. "Was Niner here copping a feel?"

Sweets laughed. "No, just a little AC/DC experiment."

"AC/DC? Cool."

"Can you walk?"

"Yeah, I think so."

"Good. Then you'd better be ready to run because everybody out there wants to kill you again."

Approaching Yangon, Myanmar

"All right!" cried Dawson as cheers, high fives, and fist bumps erupted throughout the cabin, even the CNN crew putting their impartiality aside for a brief moment with the word Red was still alive and kicking.

"Take it you got good news?" asked the pilot from the front.

Dawson stepped forward, grinning ear to ear. "Looks like our guy still had at least one of his nine lives left."

"Happy to hear it, Sergeant Major. Am I turning around?"

"Hell no. I've still got six men, two Marines, four flight crew, and seven civilians to get out of there. This day has only just begun."

The pilot pointed ahead at the river. "I can only bring you so far up this before we hit the city."

"Take us as far as you're comfortable, sir. I realize we're unescorted and this is high risk."

"Oh, you're right about it being high risk, Sergeant Major." The pilot jerked his chin to the left and right. "But you're wrong about us being unescorted."

Dawson looked forward and smiled at the sight of two Vipers that had joined them, a fact missed by all as they worried about Red. "Well, at least we won't be alone in that court-martial."

East of Dagon Tower

Yangon, Myanmar

Champo fired another burst from his assault rifle as they approached an intersection jammed with civilians. His driver hammered on the brakes and they skidded to a halt, stuck behind at least half a dozen vehicles as gunfire rattled around the corner, the drivers having apparently abandoned their cars and trucks to take cover. He smashed his fist into the dash and stepped out of the jeep, sprinting toward the action. As he pushed through the crowds desperate to escape, he rounded the corner and a bullet whipped past him that had him ducking into a small shop doorway. He leaned back out, peering down the road, assessing the situation. He spotted two Americans, their backs to him as they crossed the road, one of them helping the other. Farther down were several soldiers, including a couple with red scarves, firing wildly, none of their shots aimed as they attempted to maintain cover.

The Americans were no doubt expert shots, unlike most of those in his army, but he didn't suffer from that malady. He raised his weapon and took aim. It was time for revenge. It was time for justice to be delivered. He squeezed the trigger.

To say Red wasn't feeling himself would be an understatement. If Sweets were to be believed, he had been dead for ten minutes, give or take. However long it was, it was too long. Men's hearts weren't meant to stop, but Sweets' CPR had kept things pumping enough to, hopefully, avoid any brain damage. He was still sluggish, and wondered if it was because his body had been deprived of oxygen for so long and now that everything was flowing again, it would take time to reoxygenate all his systems. Whatever the cause, he was slowly getting better, but this was the thick of battle and he needed to be better now.

He had an arm over Sweets' shoulders as his brother-in-arms and longtime friend helped him across the street. Sweets pointed. "They went down that alleyway and they're continuing southeast. We can't be more than fifteen minutes behind them."

"Fifteen? I thought you said I was out maybe ten."

Sweets shrugged. "What do I know? I'm not a Swiss watch. I saved your—"

A shot rang out from behind them, cutting Sweets off in mid-sentence. Blood spattered across Red's face as a chunk of the side of his friend's head was blown off.

"Sweets!" cried Red as his friend crumpled to the ground. Red spun, raising his M4 and returned fire. The adrenaline surging through his system gave him his strength back and he grabbed his downed comrade, dragging him toward the alley as more gunfire erupted. He swung his M4 around, pouring lead on the previous position and managed to reach the alleyway and cover. He flipped Sweets onto his back and gasped.

He checked for a pulse but knew there would be none. There was no surviving this. The entire right side of Sweets' skull was missing, the brain exposed, shredded by bone fragments. Gunfire intensified behind him, the increase in volume indicating the enemy was emboldened, moving in on the entrance. He hoisted Sweets onto his shoulder then ran toward the opposite end. A shot rang out behind him and he turned slightly aiming his M4 behind him. He squeezed off several rounds, sending the enemy scattering, giving him enough time to reach the end and turn onto yet another street. As he continued the zigzag, south and east, south and east, he activated his comms.

"Control, Zero-Two. Zero-Nine is KIA. I repeat, Zero-Nine is KIA."

Leroux responded immediately. "Zero-Two, Control, can you confirm? You were KIA a minute ago as well."

"They blew half his head off!" Red's voice cracked. "He's dead."

"Acknowledged, Zero-Two. Where did you leave his body? We lost track of you in the alleyway."

"I'm carrying him out."

There was a pause and Dawson's voice cut in, giving him the order that he didn't want to hear, but had to be given and obeyed. "Zero-Two, Zero-One. Leave him behind. We'll recover him later. You have to save yourself, over."

Red pressed forward, the adrenaline already wearing off, his weakened body protesting with every step. "They'll hack him to pieces, BD. I can't let that happen."

Dawson's voice softened. "I hear you, brother. But there's no way he would want you dying just so that he could have an open casket. Put him down. Save yourself so you can tell his family that he died a hero and not in some bullshit training accident."

A man rushed out of a doorway to Red's right. Red swung his rifle toward him and the man held up his hands, waving them.

"Friend! Friend!" said the man repeatedly. He beckoned him through the doorway, leaving Red with a decision to be made. Did he continue forward carrying his fallen brother and get himself killed, abandon his brother to the wolves that pursued them and save his own ass, or trust a stranger who claimed to be a friend? He cursed and followed the man through the door and into a small electronics shop. It was empty save for the man and a teenage girl, her eyes wide with fear. The man said something to her and the girl's head bobbed vigorously.

"My father says you're safe here."

Red stepped deeper inside as the man closed the door and locked it. "Why are you helping me?"

"He's a member of the opposition. The government is our enemy." The man said something and the daughter continued translating. "Is your friend..."

"My friend is dead."

The girl gasped, tears filling her eyes. "I'm sorry!"

Red pointed toward the back. "I can't stay here, it's too dangerous, but I don't want to leave my friend outside. You know what they'll do to him."

She translated and her father nodded, beckoning Red to follow him through a door at the rear that led to a storage area. The man pointed at the floor, saying something to his daughter.

"He says to leave him here. You can come and get him when it's safe."

Red gently lay Sweets on the floor and carefully brushed the stray hairs off his friend's forehead. He snapped off the dog tags then placed a hand on his friend's chest and closed his eyes, begging for forgiveness for leaving him behind in enemy territory.

"Zero-Two, Zero-One, what's your status, over?"

"Momentarily secure, stand by."

The daughter left the room then reappeared a moment later with a blanket. Red took it and covered his friend's body with it then rose. The father handed him a card, saying something. Red looked to the young girl.

"This is the address and number for the shop. Have someone call us when you're ready."

Red slipped the card into a pocket then Velcroed it shut. "Thank you. If anyone asks, I left the body here against your will and said I would come back and kill you if you told anyone. Hopefully, that'll protect you."

"I'll tell him."

"Is there a back way out of here?"

She pointed at another door. "Through there. At the end of the hallway you'll come out into an alleyway."

Red shook the man's hand then the girl's. "Thank you, thank you both." He took one last look at his friend, the horror of what had taken him now hidden under the blanket, and swore he wouldn't rest until his brother lay among the honored dead at Arlington.

South of Yangon, Myanmar

Dawson hopped off the chopper and sprinted toward a nearby berm, dropping to the ground as he surveyed the area. The chopper lifted off behind him, the Vipers thundering overhead before banking in opposite directions and heading back to sea. He waved at them then took a knee, pointing toward the river just to their right.

"Let's charter a boat, gentlemen. I have no intention of walking."

The team rose then Niner smacked him on the arm, jerking a thumb behind them. "We've got company."

The lack of urgency in Niner's voice had Dawson groaning, for he knew what his friend meant. He turned to see Aynslee Kai and her cameraman standing barely twenty feet from where the chopper had landed. He cursed. "I thought I told you two to stay on the chopper."

Aynslee strode toward him. "We're not military, Sergeant Major. We can do what we want."

Dawson jabbed a finger at her. "One of my team is already dead, another almost died. Slow us down and you'll be left behind."

"We're just here to document what happens. You do your job, I'll do mine, and we'll get along just fine."

Dawson growled and turned to Niner. "You and Atlas bring up the rear. Make sure they don't slow us down."

"You got it, boss."

Atlas' voice rumbled. "Don't worry, BD. If I have to, I'll put one of them over each shoulder."

Aynslee eyed the big man. "You wouldn't dare."

Niner grinned. "Oh, he would, darling. And if he does, you're in for a treat. The man has a spectacular ass to stare at."

Dawson suppressed a smile as Aynslee took a surreptitious look. "I'll take your word for it."

Her cameraman, Roy, leaned hard to the left, tilting his head. "Looks damn fine to me."

Atlas' eyes widened and he jabbed a finger at Niner. "I get enough of that shit from him. I don't need it coming from both ends."

Niner grinned. "Oh, it'll be—"

Dawson cut Niner off. "And that has you pole vaulting over the line. Let's get a move on. I want to be at that outflow pipe in less than fifteen minutes."

Northern Shore of Inya Lake

Yangon, Myanmar

Jack handed over the last of the payment to Zeyar, the man's entire body still quaking from what he had been through. Jack pointed at the stack of cash. "I highly suggest you don't flash that around for at least a few weeks. Find a good place to hide it, and like I said before, if anybody asks, I forced you at gunpoint."

Zeyar stared at him wide-eyed. "They're going to kill me. They're going to kill my family. They're never going to believe that I didn't cooperate."

Jack drew his Glock and pointed it at Zeyar's shoulder. "I can help you with that."

Zeyar stared at him, his jaw dropping, then it snapped shut and he squeezed his eyes closed, giving a single curt nod. "Do it."

Jack squeezed the trigger, blowing a hole through the man's shoulder where it would hopefully not do too much permanent damage. It certainly wouldn't kill him.

Zeyar collapsed to the ground, shock on his face, part of him no doubt never believing Jack would actually shoot. Someone screamed from inside the small tourist operation and a woman rushed out.

"Your wife?"

Zeyar nodded as she dropped to her knees, uncertain as to what to do, screaming in Burmese at both of them.

"Tell her to apply pressure to the wound and get you to a doctor, and whatever you do, don't tell her the truth."

Zeyar winced up at him. "You want me to lie to my wife?"

Jack jerked his chin at the enraged woman glaring at him. "Look at that hatred. She'll believe anything you tell her, and so will the authorities if she's backing up your story."

Zeyar glanced over at his furious wife. "You might just be right. If I were you, I'd get out of here now before she kills you."

Jack chuckled. "It's been a pleasure doing business with you."

East of Dagon Tower

Yangon, Myanmar

Red was nauseous. Friends had died before on missions, some even under his command like Sweets was, but none were dead because of him. Sweets was dead because he had stayed behind in a desperate attempt to save his life, an attempt that had succeeded, yet the equation remained balanced. One survived, one died. Only the names changed in the report. But his best friend was right—he had to survive this so that he could tell Sweets' family why he had died, to thank them for his sacrifice, and to figure out some way to repay the impossible debt.

He reached the end of the alleyway and pressed his back against the wall. He took a swig from his canteen as he struggled to steady himself. He had a job to do, and that didn't include just saving his own skin—he had to reach his team because they were two guns down. He activated his comms. "Control, Zero-Two, do you have my location, over."

"Confirmed, Zero-Two, we've got your location and a visual. There's a laneway just opposite where you are, and at the moment, the hostiles are concentrated one street over. If you go now, you should make it, over."

"Copy that, Control." Red poked his head out, double-checking, and spotted nothing but civilians, most cowering inside doorways as gunfire continued to echo. He darted across the road, heading into the laneway, then continued to sprint the length of it.

Leroux's voice crackled in his ear. "You're still clear. When you reach the end, you'll be heading right. Hold for my command."

"Copy that." Red continued to the end then held. He peered around the corner and saw a military jeep one street over, its two-man crew with their eyes focused toward the action and not him. He checked the opposite direction, finding it clear.

"Stand by, Zero-Two, we're arranging a distraction."

Moments later, an F-18 roared overhead at full throttle, streaking across the skies, sending all eyes upward. Red bolted, making it across the street.

"Control, Zero-Two, that worked brilliantly. Let's keep that in mind, over."

"Copy that, Zero-Two. Continue down the alley then right. We'll have you reunited with your team in no time. The enemy in the immediate vicinity is concentrating their forces where you and Zero-Nine were last spotted."

Red acknowledged the report and prayed that the father and daughter that had helped him made it through unscathed.

Champo tilted his head back and roared in rage. The Americans had somehow escaped. He was certain he had killed one of them—there was no way anyone survived having the side of their head blown off, but looks could be deceiving. It might have been a glancing blow that ran along the skull and merely created a show of blood. It was the only explanation. The other man with him had carried him into the shadows of the shops where he had lost sight of them. He had to assume they had continued down the street and into an alleyway, but they had searched the area and come up empty.

He jogged back to where the enemy had been shot and pointed at the ground, positive there was a chunk of skull sitting on the pavement. "He's dead. He has to be. If he's not, the only way he's getting out of here is if he's carried out."

One of his sergeant majors frowned. "But we've searched the area, sir. There's no sign of them. And if he's carrying him, dead or alive, it has to be slowing him down."

Champo agreed and surveyed the area, at least a dozen shops within fifty paces. "Search the shops. They're the only places they could hide."

"Yes, sir."

The sergeant major snapped orders at the men and they fanned out in pairs, the search beginning anew. They would find them. They couldn't have gone far. And when he did, he would skin them alive for what they had done to his niece.

He kicked the piece of skull into the gutter then spat after it.

No quarter would be shown.

Yangon River, Myanmar

Dawson hopped in the back of the boat as Spock and Jimmy untied it from the makeshift dock. Atlas yanked the starter cord and the engine roared to life, signaling the rest to get on board as Dawson shoved the throttle forward, steering them out into the river. Somebody shouted from the shoreline, sprinting toward them. Niner raised his M4, aiming at the man but not firing. He was innocent in all this, merely the boat owner unfortunate enough to leave his prized possession unattended and in their vicinity.

"Everybody on the deck. I want to keep as low a profile as possible," ordered Dawson.

Atlas lay down as did the others, pressing against the rotting deck and below the gunnels so any casual observer from the riverbank wouldn't see them. Dawson was still visible to the naked eye, but he propped his rifle in the corner of the three-sided pilot house and pressed himself as close to the wheel as he could, lost in the shadows thrown by the sun now far in the western sky.

Two F-18s roared overhead, following the river into the city. He glanced over at the shoreline to see those on land staring up at the show of force in what could prove to be a useful distraction. He activated his comms. "Control, Zero-One. How far are we from that pipe, over?"

"You're only three klicks away, Zero-One. When you reach the split in the river, keep right, then the pipe is on your left, about two hundred meters in, over."

"Copy that, Control." Dawson peered ahead, the split in the river visible, and he prayed the sputtering engine would get them all the way as it battled the current flowing out toward the Andaman Sea.

"Get off me, little man."

Dawson glanced back to see Atlas shove Niner away from him.

"What? I just thought you'd like to cuddle."

"Drape your leg over me one more time and I'll be cuddling a corpse."

Niner batted his eyes at the big man. "I can imagine worse things."

Spock snickered. "If you think playing a corpse is a good time, I pity Angela."

Niner gave Spock the stink eye. "I'll have you know, she loves it when we play Weekend at Bernie's. Have you ever heard of rigor mortis?"

Groans was the response from everyone including Aynslee. "You do know there's a lady present?"

Atlas grunted. "You mean another lady?"

Niner rolled onto an elbow, staring dreamily at Atlas then gave Aynslee a look. "Do I have competition?"

Aynslee held up her hands. "He's all yours."

176

Niner grinned at Atlas. "You heard the lady."

Spock's eyebrow shot up. "Doesn't he get a choice in the matter?"

Dawson reached the split in the river. "That's enough, ladies. We're at the split. Two hundred meters on the left is the pipe. Everybody stays down until I say so, and be prepared for a horrendous smell. Something tells me this treatment plant isn't going to be functioning too well with the power out."

"What does that mean?" asked Aynslee.

"It means, ma'am, that you're going to regret the day you decided to become a foreign correspondent instead of sitting behind a desk."

Niner laughed. "Yeah, raw sewage is going to be getting in all our nooks and crannies."

Atlas groaned. "Lovely."

Niner rolled toward the big man, his face stopping within inches of Atlas'. "Don't worry, you big lug. I'll hose you off."

En Route to Dagon Tower

Yangon, Myanmar

Jack revved the engine of his stolen moped, the antiquated conveyance struggling to carry his Western frame and the cart attached to the back. The streets were mostly clear from the north, the crowds around the embassy still concentrated on the grounds, ransacking the building and accomplishing nothing but earning the disdain of civilized audiences, as the press back home no doubt paid them lip service by trying to explain to their audience why they were acting the way they were, then focusing in on the images they isolated of mostly men with crazed eyes, implying Myanmar's population was uncivilized and insane.

With fighter jets roaring overhead and the thunderclap of helicopters to the south, the rattling of machine guns kept most people off the streets or fleeing the scene of the action. It gave him a straight shot toward his destination—a small electronics shop holding the body of one of America's fallen warriors.

That was one thing that he liked about working alone. If the good guy were to die, it meant *he* was dead. It was something he was prepared for, and it never really bothered him as long as it wasn't a useless death. As far as he was concerned, every mission he went on, he was already dead, then if he survived, that was gravy. It meant no hesitations, no delayed reactions as he contemplated whether doing something could get him killed—it didn't matter since he was already dead, and so far his instincts had always paid off.

He was still on the right side of the dirt.

"Jackrabbit, Control. You're three hundred meters from your destination. Heavy hostile presence. Are you still sure you want to do this, over?"

It was a volunteer assignment. When he had heard what happened to Sweets and the fact the man's body had to be left behind, he immediately requested the job. The desecration the hero would suffer at the hands of his enemy was unthinkable, and if preventable, it should be, even if it meant risking his life for a dead man. If some report sealed in the bowels of Langley indicated he had died attempting to recover the body of one of America's fallen, he could live with that. That was something worth dying for, though he had no intention of dying.

Not today.

He pulled the brim of his hat down lower and made sure his facemask was high on his nose, covering as many of his Caucasian features as possible, then jammed his sunglasses against the bridge of his nose with his forefinger. "Control, Jackrabbit. I've got nothing better to do. Guide me in, over."

"Roger that, Jackrabbit. Be advised, the hostiles are searching the stores. Be prepared to encounter the enemy, over."

"Acknowledged, Control. Be advised, I intend to be the hostile in this equation, over."

There was a chuckle from the other end. "Understood, Jackrabbit. Be prepared for a left-hand turn at the roadblock ahead, then take your immediate right into the alleyway."

"Copy that, Control." Jack spotted the intersection, half a dozen troops within sight, none paying any attention to him yet. "Control, is the cellular network back up?"

"Affirmative."

"Then make the call."

"Roger that, Jackrabbit, making the call."

Jack eased up on the throttle, dramatically reducing the whine of the engine, using his momentum to carry him toward the intersection. One of the soldiers spotted him and Jack turned his head just enough to make it appear as if he weren't looking ahead and was instead checking something behind him in the cart. One of the soldiers shouted and Jack continued to slow, drifting to the left.

He spun his head forward then leaned into his turn, applying the brake before accelerating in the new direction, his cart swinging out behind him wildly as angry shouts erupted from the soldiers. "Urgent delivery, sorry!" he shouted in Burmese, the phrase provided to him by Langley before he left on this recovery operation.

He spotted the alleyway to his right and took it just as quickly. "Control, Jackrabbit. Report."

"Jackrabbit, Control. Looks like you're still good. No sign of pursuit, though I wouldn't go back out that way. They look pissed, over."

"Acknowledged, Control. I only intend to move forward. Did you make that call, over?"

"Affirmative, Jackrabbit, we made the call but there's no answer."

Jack cursed. "Understood. Keep trying. It'd be nice to know what I'm walking into. Jackrabbit, out."

He spotted the rear of the shop just ahead and applied the brakes, skidding to a halt. There were any number of reasons why the shopkeeper might not be answering his cellphone, and unfortunately, too many of them weren't good.

East of Dagon Tower

Yangon, Myanmar

Yeshe stood trembling, his hands high in the air as he stood between his daughter and the two soldiers standing in front of him, their weapons aimed at his chest. He would be terrified if it were merely two soldiers standing in front of him, but the fact they had red scarves around their necks made them all the more dangerous. They could kill anyone they wanted without consequence. He had to be extremely careful, otherwise he could be killed and his daughter as well.

Or worse.

"Where are the Americans?" snapped the sergeant in charge.

Yeshe shook his head. "I don't know. They're not here."

The sergeant stepped forward and rammed the butt of his rifle into Yeshe's stomach. He doubled over in agony then his eyes widened at a smear of blood on the floor. He faked stumbling forward and planted his foot over the evidence that would doom them.

"I swear they're not here!"

"Where did they go?"

"I don't know. We heard the shooting and we were hiding. We didn't see anything, I swear." Still hunched over, he twisted his head so he could look up at the man. "I swear, we're loyal citizens. If I knew anything, I'd tell you."

The sergeant stared at him with disdain then shoved him backward. Yeshe stumbled into his daughter, who struggled to keep him on his feet.

The man's partner pointed at the floor. "Look."

The sergeant's eyes bulged and a sneer spread. "And I suppose you're going to tell me that's your blood?"

Yeshe clamped down on his cheek hard, wincing as he tore at the skin. "That's from when you hit me."

"Bullshit."

Yeshe spat on the floor, blood and saliva rewarding his efforts as his cellphone vibrated yet again on the nearby counter.

"Nice try." The sergeant threw him to the ground then grabbed his daughter by the hair, twisting it. She screamed in pain and fear. "Where are the Americans?" The muzzle of a rifle was pressed against his daughter's chin. "Last chance or she dies."

"In the back!" cried Yeshe, his shoulders slumping in defeat. "There's just the one, the dead one. The other man's long gone. He said if we told anybody, he would come back and kill us."

"You should fear us more than you fear the Americans!" The sergeant raised his rifle butt and slammed it down on Yeshe's head. He collapsed to the ground, his world gone black, the screams of his daughter the last thing he heard.

Jack turned the knob and pulled. The door was unlocked, which suggested either he was expected, or those inside had left in a hurry. He stepped in and swiftly headed down the corridor, drawing his Glock and twisting a suppressor in place as angry shouts grew in intensity. There was a loud crack then a thump. His experienced ear told him somebody had just been cold-cocked and taken down. A young girl screamed and two men laughed.

Jack sneered. There was nothing he hated more than rapists.

He reached the end of the corridor and opened another door, the girl's cries heartbreaking. He cleared the room, frowning at the sight of a blanket-covered body that was no doubt Sweets, then gripped the knob of the door that led deeper into the store. He could take the body and leave now and no one would be the wiser. It was the mission, but he had a conscience and there was no way in hell he was letting anything happen to that poor girl.

He readied his weapon and pulled open the door slightly, peering in to see a teenage girl standing there with her hands covering her face as two Red Scarves mauled her body from either side, laughing and leering. A man lay crumpled on the ground, his chest still moving. He was alive but unconscious, and judging from the ages involved, he must be the girl's father if Red's report on the situation was accurate.

Jack pushed the door open another few inches, raising the muzzle of his weapon. He whistled. The sergeant on the left spun and his eyes bulged when he made eye contact with Jack. Jack squeezed the trigger, putting a round between the man's eyes, then immediately adjusted his aim, putting a hole through the side of the second man's head. Both collapsed to the ground mere moments apart, and Jack stepped forward, double-tapping both in the chest.

He rushed to the front door and locked it before stepping over to the counter and picking up the still-ringing phone. He smiled at the girl. "You really need to answer your phone."

The girl cowered, having receded into a back corner. "Who—who are you?"

"You can call me Jack." He jerked his chin toward the back room. "I'm here to collect a friend of mine." He dropped to a knee and checked the man's pulse. "Is this your father?"

"Yes."

"Well, he's alive." He checked the side of his head, feeling a bulge. "I suggest you get him to a hospital. Have him checked for a concussion." He fished a wad of bills out of his pocket and passed it to the girl, who took it with a trembling hand. Her eyes widened at the amount. "That should be enough to get you the proper medical care for him." He eyed the two bodies. There was no way he could leave them there—there was blood everywhere. Unfortunately, this would take time to clean up, time he didn't have.

He would have to take the riskier, though ultimately safer option.

He pointed at the girl. "Here's what you're going to do. I'm going to go take my friend. You're going to count to one hundred then you're going to go out that front door screaming for help and tell them that some white man came in here, shot the soldiers, hit your father on the head, then left."

He stepped through the pool of blood from one of his victims and walked around the shop, making a point of stepping in it again and again. He flicked his boot in it several times, sending sprays of the crimson liquid in multiple directions.

"If there was any evidence of my friends in here, it's all mixed in with their blood now. If they ask about my friends, you just say you never saw anybody. You were hiding." He pointed to the counter. "You were hiding back there. You heard somebody run through, but that was it. When you told the soldiers what you heard, I came in and shot them and hit your father. Tell them you need to get him to a hospital. Don't show them the money. Understood?"

She nodded.

"Good." Jack went back into the storage room and lifted Sweets over his shoulder. There was a pool of blood, though not large, Sweets' heart long having stopped pumping before he was even brought inside. He kneeled, taking the end of the blanket now wedged between his shoulder and Sweets' body, and wiped up the blood as best he could then stepped through it. He turned to see the girl standing in the doorway. He pointed at the bloodstain. "If they ask about this, tell them you think I got shot."

"Will you be all right?"

He smiled at her concern. "You're a good kid. I'll be fine." He handed her a card with nothing but a number on it. "If you get in trouble, you call that and leave a message for Jack."

She took the card and clasped it to her chest. "Are you Jack?"

"Yes. Now, start counting to one hundred." He winked. "But not too fast."

He headed out the opposite door and jogged down the hall. He opened the rear door to the alleyway and peered outside. It was clear. "Control, Jackrabbit. I have Zero-Nine, over." He placed the body on the cart then covered it with the blanket, tucking the handwoven heirloom tightly around the body, then hopped on the moped and started the engine. It strained as it got underway, Leroux's voice guiding him south and hopefully away from the danger.

The girl screamed behind him, and he prayed she was able to sell the story he had given her.

The last thing Sweets would have wanted was for anyone else to die because of him.

Moore/James Residence, Abbotts Park Apartments

Fayetteville, North Carolina

Maggie Harris and the bulk of the Better Halves Club were gathered at Vanessa's apartment. She slowly chewed on a Greek concoction that she would call a mini spanakopita. Vanessa wasn't giving any names for what she was feeding them. She said she didn't want anyone influenced by things they might have heard of in the past. She merely wanted their eyes, noses, and mouths to make the decision.

Maggie covered her mouth. "Oh my God, this is so good."

Niner's girlfriend Angela Henwood agreed, giving two thumbs-up as she continued to chew.

Red's wife, Shirley, groaned. "I don't know how Atlas maintains his figure with food this good around."

Vanessa beamed at them all. "I'm so glad you like it. That's one of my favorites. And as for Atlas, I think the Unit keeps him on his toes enough to burn off anything I might manage to get in him."

Maggie giggled. "That and keeping Niner at bay."

They all laughed and Angela shook her head. "I'd swear those two were star-crossed lovers if I didn't know better." She rolled her eyes. "Sometimes I'm jealous of those two. They're so close!"

"Yeah, if opposites attracted," agreed Vanessa.

Angela smirked. "Yeah, those two are about as opposite as they get. They remind me of that old TV commercial for the dog food, the one with the big bulldog and the little Jack Russell bouncing along beside it."

Maggie snorted. "Oh, my God, that's so perfect. I think that's the best description of the two of them I've ever heard."

Angela worked her phone and brought up the ad, playing it for all of them, and they roared with laughter. She swiped her thumb when it was finished and frowned.

Maggie picked up on it. "What's wrong?"

"There's a news alert. Something big is happening in Myanmar."

Maggie tensed and Angela's eyes narrowed. "What? You know something, don't you?"

Maggie turned away. "You know I'm not allowed to discuss it. I'm exposed to things because of my job that I can't share."

"To hell with that." Vanessa rushed from the kitchen and into the living room. She turned on the television and switched it to CNN then cried out. Everyone bolted, surrounding the TV to see what had shocked her.

Maggie slapped a hand over her mouth as footage on a loop showed the man she loved and his brothers she knew so well on the rooftop of the American Embassy, gunfire blazing as missiles streaked the sky, the news anchor covering the escalating situation reporting that at least one

US serviceman had lost his life. She collapsed onto the couch as she fumbled for her phone, calling the only person who might know what was going on. The call was immediately picked up.

"I was wondering when you were going to call," said her boss, Colonel Clancy.

"Is he…"

"I'm going to stop you right there. We have an active operation that at the moment is highly compartmentalized. I can't tell you anything."

"But they said one serviceman's already dead."

"If you're referring to the CNN report, that's correct. And I'll tell you this, the serviceman they're referring to was a US Marine stationed at the embassy."

Her shoulders slumped in relief, guilt overcoming her. Her fiancé was alive, her friends were alive, but someone's husband, son, or father wasn't. And if there was one thing she had learned over the years of working at Fort Bragg, it was that the entire US military was a family.

And they were all grieving now.

USS Ronald Reagan

Sea of Bengal

Louise held her arms out and her husband helped her onto the deck of the aircraft carrier. She had been on a couple of ships in her life, but never anything as big as this. It was incredible, a city on the sea, a bustle of activity surrounding her as planes took off and landed, helicopters touching down as others lifted off, men in different-colored uniforms indicating their roles rushing about as they coordinated the organized chaos.

It was a sight to behold.

And it made her proud to be an American, but also ashamed that this was all because of her.

They were led through a door then a series of corridors and finally into what could best be described as a conference room. Her husband sat her down then patted her hand. "I'll be back as soon as I can." He followed an officer from the room and someone found the remote

191

control for the television, turning it on and flipping through the channels until they found a broadcast about the unfolding situation.

Things were getting far worse.

She rubbed her eyes dry and sniffed in some strength, then turned to a young seaman standing at the door. "Excuse me, young man, but can you tell me if the others from last night are here on board?"

The man shook his head. "I'm afraid not, ma'am. I'm not privy to that information. However, when the lieutenant returns with the ambassador, I'm sure he can answer any questions you may have."

She smiled weakly at him. "Thank you. I understand." She stared at the television screen, footage from around the city shown, much of it shot by cellphones, some of it by freelance reporters, few major news organizations beyond CNN on the ground. She didn't know much about Aynslee Kai. She had seen her covering various stories around the world, of course, but her exposure to her today had impressed her. She had kept a level head through the entire situation, had obeyed orders when it was prudent to do so, and according to what she was hearing, had gone back into the thick of things to follow the story, the CNN anchor expressing concern that they couldn't establish contact with her.

"I hope they're okay," said someone, she didn't know who. Everything was still a fog. She clasped her hands in front of her then closed her eyes and recited the Lord's Prayer for the brave men and women putting their lives on the line for strangers, for countrymen, for each other.

Oh, God, forgive me for what I've done.

Southeast of Dagon Tower

Yangon, Myanmar

The nausea was gone and Red was back to feeling 100%, or at least as close to it as he could expect after his knock on Heaven's door had gone unanswered. He sprinted down yet another alleyway, reaching the end of it, sucking in air as every muscle in his body was spent. His time alone had given him the opportunity to come up with a theory as to why he felt like a raw recruit on his first day of Basic. Every single muscle in his body must have tensed with the shock Sweets had used to bring him back, and his stored energy had been depleted. It would take some time, and certainly lots of fluids to get back to normal.

And some food.

He tore off another chunk of the energy bar he had been working on for the past couple of minutes after he had recognized what was happening to him. It was working. It had settled his stomach, but he needed a break.

You'll rest when you're dead.

His comms squawked. "Zero-Two, Control. Thought you would like to know that Jackrabbit has recovered Zero-Nine and is headed for the coast. Hopefully, we'll have him in international waters inside half an hour, over."

Red gave a fist pump in celebration of the news and smiled. "Acknowledged, Control. Pass on my thanks to Jackrabbit, over."

"Will do, Zero-Two."

Heavy gunfire nearby ended the celebration.

"Control, report."

"Your unit's taking heavy fire one street over to your southeast, over."

"Copy that, Control. I'm on my way." Red peered out to make sure it was clear then sprinted down the street and into another alleyway. The gunfire grew louder and muzzle flashes punctuated the shadows ahead. He slowed, not wanting to run headlong into an enemy position. He removed his sunglasses so he could see better, and spotted two of the enemy were at the opposite end, firing to his right. He could hear M4s responding to the AK-47s. The fire was near continuous from both sides.

The situation was desperate.

He stopped, raised his weapon, and put two rounds into the back of the man on the left, then two more into the man on the right, silencing their weapons. He rushed forward, reaching the downed position, and poked his head out. "This is Zero-Two. Friendly to your north in the alleyway, over."

Jagger responded. "It's about time you showed up, Zero-Two. Care to lend us a hand?"

"With pleasure." Red took aim at the opposite side of the street where two hostiles continued to spray lead on his friends. Four more disciplined rounds had two more down.

"North clear," announced Jagger.

Red scanned the area to confirm. "Friendly coming in from the north," he reported, then stepped into the street, sprinting toward his team's position at a crouch, gunfire from ahead still spraying the area. He came to a halt beside Jagger, taking cover behind a shot-up truck.

Jagger grinned at him and gave him an elbow to the ribs. "Thought you were a goner."

"Apparently I was. But we lost Sweets."

Jagger grimaced, the pain in his eyes evident. "We'll mourn him later, brother."

Red gave him a nod and activated his comms. "Control, Zero-Two back in command. Give me a sit rep, over."

"Zero-Two, Control. Enemy forces are concentrating to the south in an effort to cut off any escape. The sewage treatment plant is less than half a klick from your current position, still to the southeast. If you can get in there, you should be able to rendezvous with Zero-One's team, then it's a straight shot out to the river, over."

"Copy that, Control. Let's get this shitshow underway." He turned to Jagger. "Where are the civilians?"

Jagger pointed to his left. "The rest of the team's in there, securing the opposite end."

"Okay. Let's fall back to the alleyway entrance. Maintain suppression fire until I can see what's going on at the other end."

Jagger opened fire and Red darted into the alley. He slapped Mickey on the back. "Suppression fire."

"You got it. Good to have you back."

Red hurried down the narrow lane, checking on each civilian as well as the Marines and aircrew. He paused at the woman who had taken a round to the shoulder. "How are you holding up, ma'am?"

She gave him a weak thumbs-up. "I'm still alive."

He laughed. "Then you're doing better than I was a few minutes ago. Just a little while longer, and we'll have you out of here."

"Looking forward to it."

He reached the end where Casey had engaged the enemy. "Report."

"We've got half a dozen about fifty meters down the road with a fifty in an up-armored vehicle. We're not getting past them, not without some help."

Red took a peek and cursed. "Then how about we get that help."

East of Dagon Tower

Yangon, Myanmar

"Help us! Please help us!"

Champo spun and spotted a young woman erupt from a small shop, her hands in the air, terror on her face as she rushed toward two of his men. He strode swiftly toward her. "What's going on?"

She pointed a shaking finger at the store. "An American, he came in and killed two soldiers and hit my father. He needs help!"

He bristled and indicated for his men to come with him as he sprinted toward the open door. He rushed inside and cursed at the sight of two of his men in a heap on the floor, pools of blood beside both of them, one with a shot directly between the eyes. It was an expert kill. The girl's father lay nearby, groaning.

He turned to the girl. "What happened?"

She pointed at the counter. "My father and I were hiding back there then we heard something that sounded like people coming through. I think they went out the back. When your soldiers came in looking for them, a man came in from the back and shot your two men then hit my father on the head before leaving."

"This man, was he a soldier?"

She shrugged. "I don't know. I guess so."

"Was he wearing a uniform?"

Her eyes narrowed. "No, I don't think so, but I can't be sure. All I could see was the gun."

"Why didn't he kill you?"

"I'm not a threat, maybe?"

Champo headed through the door at the rear of the shop, following the bloody footprints. There was a smear of blood in the corner of the storage room and more footprints. He pointed at the bloodstain, leaning back so he could see the girl. "What about this?"

She stepped to the door and her eyebrows shot up. "I don't know. Maybe he was shot by one of your men?"

Champo pursed his lips, not so sure. He hadn't been far from the store the entire time and was sure he would have heard an AK-47 firing from so close, though perhaps not. There was gunfire all around the city right now, and perhaps a single round might have escaped his notice. He followed the prints down the hallway and out into the alley. Little light made it past the mishmash of awnings overhead, but it was clear even in this light that the footprints ended here, which meant the Americans must have had a vehicle waiting.

He spotted a soldier to his right and whistled, beckoning him over. The man spotted the red scarf and his eyes bulged. He wasted no time in obeying his order.

"Yes, Captain?"

"Did you see anybody come in this alleyway in the past five minutes?"

"Just a delivery guy on a motorcycle."

"You let him in?"

The corporal's jaw slackened slightly. "Not exactly, sir. He blew through our checkpoint by accident. He shouted that he had an urgent delivery and was sorry, then went up here. We radioed in for instructions on what to do, but we can't get through. The radios are jammed."

Champo cursed. The Americans had taken out the power and the phone networks, and must be jamming their radio frequencies as well. "What did he look like?"

The corporal shrugged. "I didn't get a really good look at him, sir. Ball cap, sunglasses, facemask, just like any other delivery driver these days."

"So, he was on a motorcycle and he was alone?"

"Yes."

"Dressed like a local?"

"Yes. Oh, and he had a cart behind him."

"Cart?"

"Yeah, maybe two meters long, one meter wide, probably carrying whatever he was delivering."

Champo cursed again, examining where the footprints ended. There was a distinct tread mark from a tire visible in the grime. This was how they had escaped, but it was the timing that didn't make sense. He had shot the American, then they had disappeared. It had been at least ten minutes between when that had happened and the girl had rushed out of the shop. The Americans would have had to go through her shop while she and her father were hiding. He was certain he had killed one of them, and that they were both wearing Special Forces gear.

So, who was the man on the motorcycle? Was he nobody, merely someone making a delivery as they claimed, or was he part of this? Was he the man who came in and shot his soldiers and pistol-whipped the father? The story from the girl's perspective could still be true. The Americans went through the shop and out the back, one of them possibly dead, carried by his comrade. The father and daughter emerge from hiding, having not seen anything. A few minutes later, his soldiers go in, the delivery driver comes through the back, shoots them, cold-cocks the father, leaves, and the girl runs outside for help.

It all still fit, but he had his doubts. Something didn't add up. Why were there so many bloody footprints? Why was there a smudge in the storage room? Had there been another pool of blood there? And why would a third man return? His mouth widened with the realization of what had occurred, and he smiled slightly. He *had* killed the American. His partner had carried him through the store and left the body in the storage room then escaped out the back. Someone else, perhaps CIA, perhaps a traitor, came in to recover the body but encountered his men, so shot them. Did he hit the father because he was a loyal citizen attempting to stop the American, or perhaps his men discovered the body first and struck down the father as a collaborator?

Something was going on. He was sure of it. He had two collaborators on his hands, two collaborators who might know something that could lead him to the Americans or at a minimum deserved punishment for having helped them escape.

He faced the corporal. "Have everyone at the roadblock write down exactly what they saw. Describe the man, his motorcycle, and his cart, then report back to me. Captain Champo."

"Yes, sir." The man rushed back toward his checkpoint and Champo returned inside to find his men arguing over what the bloodstain in the storage room could mean.

"He was shot, like she said."

"She didn't say he was shot. She said *maybe* he was shot."

"How could she not know? Wouldn't she have heard it?"

"Our guys were shot six times. How did we not hear that? We were just outside."

"Well, I didn't hear it and you didn't hear it, so maybe we didn't hear our guys shooting either."

Champo chewed his cheek as he listened and puzzled out the problem. "He was using a silencer," he said.

Both men spun toward him and snapped to attention, the corporal responding. "Yes, sir. That would make sense, though it wouldn't explain why we didn't hear our men shooting back."

"Because they didn't."

Both men's eyes bulged. "What do you mean? What about this blood?" asked the private.

"I think it belongs to the man I shot earlier. I think his body was kept here until the third man was able to retrieve it."

"Third man?"

Champo didn't have time to explain, instead pushing past them back into the shop. The girl had questions to answer and he was determined to find out what she knew. He froze, his head darting from left to right, the father and daughter nowhere in sight. "Where the hell did they go?"

His two men stumbled forward, both forcing their way through the door at the same time. Neither said anything, their mouths merely agape.

"Why weren't you two idiots watching them?"

The private's eyes darted to the ground. "I...I..."

The corporal spoke. "We didn't think they were going anywhere. He was barely conscious and she was on the floor beside him. There was no reason to think she would leave him alone. I can't believe he was able to get to his feet."

Champo raised his AK-47 and put two rounds in the corporal's stomach. The man doubled over then hit the floor, his own blood adding to the mix. The private snapped to attention, his eyes wide, his bottom lip trembling as his jaw slammed shut. "Let that be a lesson to you, Private. Failure is not tolerated by those who wear the red scarf. Now, let's find that girl. She obviously knows something."

En Route to the Shwe Baho Hospital

Yangon, Myanmar

Eindra leaned forward, twisting the throttle of her scooter as she stood on the running board, her father perched on the seat behind her, his head leaning on her back, his hands loosely gripping her waist as he struggled to remain conscious. In a moment of lucidity, she had helped him to his feet as the soldiers debated the source of the blood in the storage room. She managed to get him outside and onto her scooter parked out front. She was now heading toward the hospital, for her father was in definite need of a doctor.

The soldiers were waving her through, eager to get civilians out of the way, and for the moment it appeared they might make it. The question was, what happened after that? Had the soldiers believed her story? If they hadn't, then the moment they returned to their shop, they would be arrested, tortured, and imprisoned, perhaps even worse. But they had to return to the shop. It was the family business. Everything they had was tied up in it. And if they didn't return, where would they go? They couldn't hide forever, and they couldn't put their family at risk by staying with them.

She carefully rounded a corner and her heart leaped into her throat when she spotted a roadblock ahead. There was no avoiding it. She couldn't turn around—it would just raise suspicions. She rode up to it and came to a halt.

"State your business," said one of the soldiers as another slowly rounded the bike.

She looked over her shoulder at her father. "He was injured by one of the Americans. The bastard struck him on the head with his gun. I'm taking him to the hospital."

"You saw the Americans?" The man seemed excited by this.

"One of them."

"Where?"

She pointed back toward the shop. "Just a couple of streets over."

"Which way were they heading?"

"I'm not sure. Away from here. They must be trying to get to the river."

The soldier cursed. "I knew we wouldn't see any action here." He looked at her father. "He doesn't look well." He indicated for the roadblock to be removed then waved her through. "Get him to the hospital. Tell them one of the American pigs did this. You'll get better service."

She flashed a smile. "Thank you." She gently accelerated past the soldiers, her heart racing. She rounded another corner and her father's head lifted off her back.

204

"You're a very brave girl." His voice sounded slightly stronger than it had a few minutes ago. She smiled back at him.

"And apparently, you're a very good actor."

He rested his head against her once again. "Not that good, unfortunately. Let's just get to that hospital."

Operations Center 3, CIA Headquarters

Langley, Virginia

Leroux rose as Morrison entered the room. "Sitrep."

"Sir, all of last night's evacuees and the one casualty have arrived at Ramstein where they're being debriefed and examined again. Repatriation should happen tomorrow morning. Dawson's group, including the ambassador and his wife, are on board the USS Ronald Reagan. Their transport will be leaving within the hour. As you're aware, we lost Sergeant Donald Peters after he managed to save Master Sergeant Belme's life. Red has rejoined his team and they're less than two hundred meters from the sewage treatment plant."

"And Dawson?"

Leroux rolled his eyes. "You know him and his team, sir. They ordered their chopper to turn back and they're attempting to reach the outflow pipe we identified earlier."

Morrison cursed. "My God, a lot can happen in half an hour."

"Yes, sir."

Morrison stared at the tactical display indicating all the assets in play. He pointed. "What are the F-18s doing?"

"Combination of roles, sir. They're making sure the enemy doesn't launch any aircraft, and they're also taking out any radar-guided weapons systems that go active, as well as any units moving into the city. They're also proving a nice distraction for those on the ground as they look up at the sky rather than down at the ground where our people are."

"And the helicopters?"

"We've got Vipers on continuous rotation from the carrier group. They're providing ground support and taking out targets of opportunity in the vicinity of our people."

"What about civilians? Rules of Engagement are not to fire if civilians might be injured."

"Well, most have fled the area already or are hiding inside. Casualties should hopefully be minimized from our side. That's not to say the enemy is doing likewise."

"What do you think their chances are?"

"Fifty-fifty at best, sir. The Burmese are moving everything they've got to the south of the city. They know where our people are heading. It's a race against time and unfortunately our people are losing it. Right now, we're assuming they're going to be able to reach the sewage treatment plant then gain access to that outflow pipe that'll take them to the river where Dawson's team has a boat waiting. If they do, then they have to get that boat back down the river into the ocean and into international waters, or we have to go in and recover them by helicopter. That would involve at least three Super Hueys. The Black Hawks are just too slow with all the RPGs flying around. It's a miracle we haven't lost any of the Vipers yet, though a few of them have come back with bird strike damage."

Morrison chuckled at the Cuban Missile Crisis reference. He stared at the screen, his hands on his hips. "So, this is what a Charlie Foxtrot looks like."

"And it could get far worse before it starts to get better."

"*If* it gets better," muttered Child as he spun in his chair.

Morrison regarded him. "Have faith, son. Those are the best of the best out there."

"Yeah, and one's dead and one *was* dead."

Morrison frowned but didn't say anything else to Child, the young man still not accustomed to losing someone on a mission. It's not that it didn't bother Leroux anymore, it was that he knew to keep his mouth shut about it so it didn't affect team morale. He would mourn the loss later when he got the rest of them home safely.

And right now, his ability to do so was in question.

Morrison lowered his voice slightly. "Speaking of Sweets…"

Leroux pointed at the display. "Jack's got him. Orange indicator."

"Does he know he's running into a wall of red?" asked Morrison, referencing the enemy targets.

"Oh, he's aware. I think the better question is, does he care?"

Heading South

Yangon, Myanmar

Jack continued south, barreling through alleyways as much as possible, one of Leroux's people in his ear guiding him toward the coast. He didn't have far to go now as the crow flew, but unfortunately for the crow, it was hunting season and his foes were sporting .50 cals.

They weren't playing fair.

A voice squawked in his ear. "Jackrabbit, Control. We just intercepted a transmission with your description indicating you're heading south, over."

"Acknowledged, Control. They were bound to put two and two together eventually. Any indication it's affected deployment, over?"

"Negative, Jackrabbit. You're still approaching the red wall. At your current rate, you should be hitting it in approximately two minutes, over."

"Copy that, Control. Wish us luck, and if I make it through, my pickup better be on time, over."

"Roger that, Jackrabbit. Your pickup is holding offshore. They'll be there. Don't you worry."

Jack grinned up at the eye in the sky. "What? Me worry? You should know me by now. I never worry."

"Then don't worry about this," responded Leroux. "After you clear the next alley, there's a technical with a fifty cal and six troops blocking your way."

"Acknowledged. Where's the nearest position to their east and west?"

"They're blocking every street and alleyway. Fifty meters to the west, forty to the east."

Jack slowed, not only to give himself time to think, but to reduce the volume of the whining engine. "Is the alleyway wide enough for the technical to go through?"

"Stand by." Leroux came back a moment later. "Affirmative, but you might lose the mirrors."

"Not to worry. My gold card includes rental insurance. I'm sure they accept it here in Myanmar. Can you tell me if it's running or if the keys are in the ignition?"

"Stand by…Infrared from the drone shows exhaust is venting. The vehicle is running."

"Understood. Stand by, Control." The end of the narrow lane was ahead and he could see the back end of the pickup truck blocking his way, two soldiers standing guard at the rear. Jack turned off the engine then climbed off the moped. He screwed the suppressor back in place on his Glock and put a spare mag in his left hand and another in Sweets' rear pants pocket then glanced up at the heavens.

How about you do me a solid today, God, and get me through this so I can get him home?

He picked up Sweets' body and slung it over his shoulder, then strode forward, his weapon extended in front of him, and added one more thought to his prayer.

Sorry about the killing I'm about to do.

He emerged into the sunlight and fired from left to right, one shot in each of the six targets, all startled and dead before they had a chance to act. Somebody shouted from his left, his ambush not going unnoticed as he rolled Sweets into the truck bed. He jumped behind the wheel and put it in gear then hammered on the gas, twisting the wheel to the left, heading for the opposite alleyway.

He emptied his mag at the targets to the east then reloaded and did the same to the west, aiming for their engine blocks rather than their personnel. He pressed the accelerator into the floor, the tires spinning before gaining traction, then within moments he was under the protection of the narrow lane. The mirrors scraped along the walls, bending inward the farther he got, and he was wondering if Langley's assessment was correct.

Could he fit through this all the way, or had their analysis only included his ability to enter?

He shifted to second, floored it, then to third, gaining more speed, smashing through debris and goods stored in the alleyway as the sunlight grew at the far end, the proverbial light at the end of the tunnel indeed growing. Gunfire erupted behind him, bullets whipping past, some slamming into the tailgate of the truck. He ducked, keeping his head as low as he could, staring at the narrow passageway ahead through the top of the steering wheel and the dash. The gunfire continued. All it would take was one lucky shot.

He reached up and adjusted the rearview mirror so he could see out the back. They were on foot, which suggested he had successfully taken out the two closest vehicles, but that .50 cal swinging wildly in the back would have made a huge difference. It was too bad Sweets couldn't man it.

He burst into the sunlight and hammered on the brakes, cranking the wheel to the right then took a rapid left onto another street, the first laneway he spotted far too narrow. The gunfire faded in the distance, but that wouldn't last long.

Nobody outran a radio.

Shwe Baho Hospital

Yangon, Myanmar

Eindra came to a halt in front of the hospital's main doors. "Help me! Help me!" she cried and two orderlies took notice.

"What's wrong?" asked one of them as they rushed over.

"My father, he was hurt by the Americans." She hated to lie, especially knowing what her father believed in, but the soldier at the checkpoint was right—the people here were more likely to help him if they thought he was a victim of the government's current enemy.

"What happened to him?"

"He was hit in the head by a rifle butt."

The two men helped her father off the scooter and into a wheelchair. One of them pointed off to the side. "Put your scooter over there. You can't leave it here."

She guided it out of the way, which was when she finally noticed the chaos that surrounded her. Scores of people were stumbling in on their own, others helped like her father. In the distance, she could hear gunfire and explosions. If this was war, it was as horrifying as her father had described it, but she would gladly suffer it if it meant freedom for her country. Unfortunately, that wasn't what this was about. The Americans were here only temporarily, rescuing their own people. Once they were done, they would be gone, then the military would reign once again with an iron fist, the democratic leaders the country so desperately wanted in power left to languish in prison.

She parked her scooter and turned back toward the entrance, panic setting in when she couldn't see her father. She rushed toward the doors and pushed inside through the crowds. "Father!" she cried, but there was no response. She stepped onto the arm of a chair, balancing against the doorframe, and stared out across the crowd. "Father!" she shouted again.

"Over here!"

Her head spun toward the voice and she spotted one of the orderlies waving at her. She hopped down and navigated through the crowd, finally reaching her father as a doctor assessed him. The man glanced over his shoulder at her. "Are you the daughter?"

"Yes, sir."

"He took a blow to the head?"

"Yes. One of the Americans hit him with the end of his rifle."

"How long was he unconscious?"

"Maybe five minutes, I'm not sure. Everything was happening so fast. It might have been longer. I really don't know."

"Well, he seems to know who he is and where he is. I suggest you take him home, put an ice pack on the bump and give him acetaminophen or ibuprofen for the pain. Don't let him sleep for the next twelve hours. If he's still having problems tomorrow, bring him in. Right now, I've got an ER filled with people who are truly at risk."

"But he's going to be all right?"

The doctor rose. "He should be. Like I said, just keep an eye on him and bring him back if he gets worse or if he's not better by tomorrow."

"Is there a Yeshe in here?" shouted somebody.

Her pulse pounded at the mention of her father's name. The question was, did they know his full name?

"Is there a Yeshe here who owns the Golden Way electronics shop?"

Her heart nearly stopped at the mention of their family business.

They had found them.

The doctor's eyes narrowed. "Wait a minute. Didn't he say his name was Yeshe?" Both orderlies shrugged. The doctor turned to the daughter. "Just what's going on here?"

The blood drained from her face and she felt faint. The doctor reached out and grabbed her by the arm, steadying her.

"Why are they after your father?"

"I-I don't know. The Americans killed some soldiers at my father's shop and they were questioning us. I left with my father to get him here without their permission, so maybe that's why."

The doctor frowned. "If they think your father's trying to hide something, they could try to beat it out of him. With his head injury, that could kill him." He pointed at a nearby set of doors then turned to the orderlies. "Get them out the back."

Both young men exchanged concerned glances but the doctor was having none of their hesitation.

215

"We're medical professionals first, loyal citizens to the government second. If the girl's story is true, they've done nothing wrong. You know how things are." Both men nodded, one of them getting behind the wheelchair. The doctor turned to her. "Get out of here now, and I suggest you don't go home. Go somewhere else where they won't think to look for you until your father's better."

She gave a weak smile. "Thank you, Doctor." She followed the orderlies through the doors as the soldiers continued to call out her father's name. As the door swung closed behind her, the doctor called to them.

"Who did you say you're looking for?"

"A man named Yeshe."

Eindra paused, pressing an ear against the door.

"He was here a few minutes ago. I already discharged him. Mild concussion. Apparently, an American soldier pistol-whipped him."

She breathed a sigh of relief then raced after her father and the orderlies, the resistance to the regime alive and well through acts of kindness as she had just witnessed.

Yangon River

Yangon, Myanmar

Dawson positioned their commandeered boat next to the outflow pipe as Niner and Atlas sprang to their feet and tied them off. Raw sewage poured into the river, the treatment plant failing to do its job with the power out. Those operating it had obviously engaged a manual override to simply send the untreated water through.

It was disgusting.

He could honestly say that at this moment, he couldn't imagine anything that could smell worse than this.

Niner grimaced. "I think I can literally taste it."

"Mask up," ordered Dawson, reaching for his gas mask and fitting it in place. What they were dealing with likely wasn't dangerous, but it could prove distracting.

Aynslee Kai cleared her throat. "Do you have any spares?"

"Sorry, ma'am. You're going to have to stay here or grin and bear it. I can't have any of my men unable to breathe freely."

She frowned but agreed. "I understand, Sergeant Major, but we're still coming with you."

Her cameraman, Roy, hurled over the railing and Niner laughed.

"I don't know if your crew is in agreement."

Dawson turned to Sergeant Zach "Wings" Hauser. "As soon as we're inside, cast off and hold position just upriver. Try to keep a low profile."

"No problem, BD. I'll be ready for you."

Aynslee was at Roy's side, the man an interesting shade of green and yellow. "Are you sure you're up for this?" He gave an unconvincing nod then dry heaved over the gunnel again.

Wings tossed him a proverbial life preserver. "I could use a second hand here, if you can spare him."

Dawson was certain Aynslee saw through Wings' offer but she showed her compassion and patted Roy on the back.

"I think that's a good idea. You stay here and help him. I'll go in with them."

Roy agreed. "You know how to work the camera?"

"Of course I do, but I'll just record with my phone. I might know how to use it, but running through sewage with one is your area of expertise, not mine. I'll lose my balance and fall in this shit."

Dawson stepped into the pipe and held out a hand to her. "If you're coming, you're coming now."

She squeezed Roy's forearm briefly then stepped into the pipe with the rest of Bravo Team. Wings untied the lines and the boat's engine revved, the bow disappearing from sight as Dawson pressed forward, deeper into the stench, thanking God they had planned ahead and brought the masks in the event tear gas was deployed.

Atlas groaned as they trudged forward. "I think I'm going to have to burn my uniform and kit."

"Me too," agreed Niner. "Not to mention the fact we're probably going to have to shower for three days straight just to remove the stench from our pores." He elbowed Atlas. "Don't worry, big guy, I can help you with all those hard-to-reach nooks and crannies."

"Careful, little man, or I'll use you as my loofah."

Niner squeaked. "Promise?"

Dawson rolled his eyes. "You walked into that one."

Atlas sighed. "I know. I have to learn not to respond."

Wings' voice came through Dawson's earpiece. "Zero-One, One-Two, we're moored one hundred meters north of the entrance. Just give us sixty seconds' notice and we'll be in position, over."

"Acknowledged, One-Two. Hopefully, we'll be seeing you soon. Zero-One, out."

Niner cursed ahead. "This wasn't in the briefing."

Dawson pushed forward. "What?"

"I don't think they like uninvited guests."

Metal on metal rattled. Atlas, blocking Dawson's view, stepped aside, revealing a grate blocking their way. Dawson cursed and activated his comms. "Control, Zero-One. We've got a problem."

Operations Center 3, CIA Headquarters

Langley, Virginia

Leroux peered at the feed from Dawson's camera. Metal bars crisscrossed the pipe, blocking any means of access, something not indicated in the plans.

"Can't they just blow it?" asked Child from his station.

Tong shook her head. "If they did, it could give away their position."

"What choice do they have? They have to get through. This has been the whole point of what Red's team has been working toward."

"Control, how far are we from the plant?" asked Dawson.

"You're only fifty meters in. You're almost half a kilometer from where we estimate the start of the pipe is."

"Control, what's Zero-Two's ETA at the plant, over?"

Leroux turned to Tong. "As little as five minutes," she replied. "They're just waiting for an airstrike that's coming in now."

Leroux passed on the update. "As little as five minutes."

"Acknowledged. As soon as they engage at the plant, let us know and we'll blow this gate. Hopefully, the action outside will cover up anything we're doing in here, over."

"Copy that, Zero-One. Stand by for our notification. "

"Acknowledged. Zero-One, out."

Leroux turned to the room. "Has anybody managed to find plans for that facility yet? I'd like to be able to tell Red how to get to that outflow pipe before he gets there." Heads shook around the room except for Packman, who raised his hand.

"I haven't been able to find plans for *this* facility, but on a hunch, I checked to see what other facilities the company had built. If you remember, it was contracted out to a Chinese firm. Well, they've built a bunch of these as part of their Belt and Road Initiative and they all appear to be identical."

Leroux excitedly urged him on with a twirling of his hand. "And?"

"And I got plans for one that was built in Pakistan." Packman tapped at his keyboard then indicated the massive displays. Leroux turned to see blueprints. A large red circle appeared as Packman explained. "If I'm not mistaken, these are the outflow pipes."

Leroux chewed his cheek for a moment. "That's showing three pipes. Ours is only showing one."

Packman frowned. "I know. That's why I hadn't said anything yet because I'm trying to figure out why."

Child spun in his chair. "What says all three pipes have to go in the same direction? Maybe they split off so that everything isn't coming out in one spot."

Leroux stared at the blueprints. Superficially, they appeared to match the footprint of the Myanmar facility in every way, the only discrepancy the pipes. "Okay, Danny, start checking the river to the north, see if there are any other outflow pipes that could explain this discrepancy. I want to have confidence I'm giving our people accurate information."

"Yes, sir. I'm on it."

Leroux returned to Tong. "Put three more on it. We're only minutes away from needing that info."

"Yes, sir." She gestured at the tactical display. "Airstrikes are coming in now."

Approaching the Sewage Treatment Facility

Yangon, Myanmar

Red glanced back at the civilians huddled against the wall in the alleyway as heavy fire came at them from both directions ahead, tearing apart the entranceway. "This is it, people, this is what we've been waiting for. As soon as I give the go order, everybody's on their feet and following Jagger." He slapped his friend on the back.

Jagger grinned, pursing his massive lips and pointing at them. "Just follow these babies. They'll lead the way."

"Zero-Two, Control, bombing run commencing now, over."

"Acknowledged, Control." Red took a knee and everyone hunched over. Multiple F-18s streaked by overhead and the ground shook as their ordnance tore apart their targets, not only behind them but ahead, clearing a path the remaining distance to the treatment plant supposed to give them a clear shot to the river.

Debris rained down from overhead as plaster crumbled and shingles broke free. The ground stopped rumbling, indicating the strikes were over, and Red rose, sprinting to the street. He checked left then right, confirming both positions had been destroyed.

"Zero-Two, Control, stand by for bomb damage assessment, over."

"Acknowledged, Control." He turned to the others. "Everybody up!" His ragtag team scrambled to its feet as he held a fist high over his head, waiting for the all-clear. "Zero-Two, Control, all targets between your position and the treatment plant have been confirmed destroyed, over."

"Copy that, Control. Heading out now." He stepped into the open. "Let's go, people!" he shouted to the others then took point, heading out into the street and toward one of the bombed-out positions. They passed a destroyed vehicle and he spotted a survivor propped up against a nearby wall. The man reached for his gun and Red put two in his chest. He kept advancing, Mickey at his side as Jagger led the civilians, the Marines and flight crew covering them as the rest of Red's team brought up the rear.

They ducked down another laneway then emerged to a sight that brought a smile. The sewage treatment plant lay just ahead, a shining beacon of modernity dropped in the middle of squalor, Myanmar and Chinese flags flying at the entrance.

Mickey stood beside him, covering his arc. "Never thought I'd be so happy to see a Chinese flag."

Red grunted. "Me neither. Clear left."

"Clear right."

Red glanced back at everyone. "This is it, people. We're almost home free."

An engine roared down the street and Red cursed at the sight of two troop transports racing toward them. If they reached the treatment plant first, his team might never make it inside. Red raised his M4 and charged forward, opening fire on the lead transport as Mickey did the same.

They weren't home free yet.

Outside the Shwe Baho Hospital

Yangon, Myanmar

Eindra strolled as casually as she could toward her scooter, still parked near the entrance of the hospital, the soldiers from minutes before out front calling her father's name.

"Yeshe, please identify yourself. We're only here to get your statement, you're not under arrest!"

She huffed.

Yeah, right.

One of the many problems in Myanmar under the junta was the fact you didn't need to be arrested for them to take you in for questioning. The questioning almost always meant torture, because the innocent telling the truth never gave the answers the army wanted. Only under torture would someone lie and tell their interrogator what they wanted to hear. She was certain it was true in all societies that allowed it. It was why those who believed in it were mistaken in how effective it was, always pointing at the changed responses they received, never acknowledging that many of those responses were the fiction, not the original honest answers. If the soldiers got their hands on her and her father, they would never be seen again.

She reached her scooter and started the engine as she mounted it. She carefully maneuvered through the crowd, desperate not to draw any attention. She had no idea what had happened after the doctor told his lie to cover their escape. Someone could have mentioned her, what she looked like, how she had arrived. Anything was possible, and when a society lived under terror of torture, they were often cooperative when it came to things that would have no impact on their personal lives or those of their friends and family. Ratting out a stranger meant they wouldn't be paid attention to, and they could get on with their day.

She made it down to the main road that ran in front of the hospital then continued to the bench she had left her father on. Her heart leaped into her throat when she spotted him lying down instead of sitting up. She came to a halt directly in front of him and stepped off her scooter. She shook him by the shoulder. "Father, are you awake?"

He groaned.

"You're not allowed to sleep."

"But I'm so tired. Just let me sleep a little bit."

She hauled him upright. "Get on your feet." It was a demand, not a request. He moaned but didn't resist as she struggled to help him up. People were looking now, and it wouldn't be long before soldiers would be coming by. He shuffled over to the scooter then sat. She climbed on and they pulled away, his head slumping once more against her back.

She had to get him to someone who could help. She couldn't go to family because that could get them in trouble. Friends might be too scared to help. She gasped as a thought occurred to her, and twisted the throttle, accelerating toward the south of the city, toward the danger, but toward the only person she could think of who could help.

Heading South

Yangon, Myanmar

Jack steered the stolen pickup truck along a beach that had never seen a tourist, judging from the debris strewn about. He spotted the Zodiac just ahead as promised, half a dozen Marines in covering fire positions, one of them beckoning toward him. He gave a couple of hammers on the horn so they knew he had spotted them then continued his battle to reach them. He caught a glance in his rearview mirror and cursed as two technicals behind him, both lucky enough to have someone in the back manning their .50 cals, came into view.

Muzzle flashes were accompanied by bullets tearing through the air and at the ground around him, some finding their mark. If his luck didn't hold out, one of those bullets would tear him a new hole, and he was most decidedly against that idea, quite happy with the number of holes he had been born with, thank you very much.

The Marines opened fire ahead of him. He didn't bother ducking. He had faith in their training and he had to see what was directly ahead.

There were far too many stray logs, tree stumps, and large rocks hidden in the sand to afford him the luxury of cover. A bullet tore through his rear window, shards of glass spraying across the back of his neck. He winced but didn't bother checking for damage. If there were, running his hands blindly through glass shards embedded in his body would only do more harm than good. Blood trickled down his back and he just prayed he had enough time left in him to reach the Zodiac so Sweets had a chance to rest in peace on home soil among his comrades-in-arms.

He checked over his shoulder as more guns thundered behind him and cursed. He might make it to the Zodiac, but the Zodiac was never making it off the beach.

A Marine dropped as if to confirm his thought when he spotted something on the horizon and smiled. Four Viper attack helicopters were rapidly approaching, missiles streaking from their weapons pods. Explosions erupted behind him but he didn't pay them any mind. He had one final job to do, and that was to cover the last fifty yards between him and that Zodiac. Blood continued to flow down his back, soaking his shirt, though he didn't sense any weakness yet. The gunfire behind him settled as the enemy were either dead or struggling to survive the onslaught from the US Navy's response.

It was only thirty yards now, and he eased off the gas as the downed Marine was carried into the back of the Zodiac, his wince indicating he was only wounded, hopefully not critically. Jack slammed on the brakes and the Marines surged forward, taking up covering positions around the vehicle, continuing to pour fire on the severely diminished enemy. Jack climbed out and stumbled to his knees, the adrenaline keeping him going failing him now that the end was in sight. He was no longer responsible for Sweets' repatriation. He had done his job, and if he died here now, it would have been worth it.

One of the crew from the boat dropped beside him. "Are you all right, sir?"

"Don't worry about me. Just get him. He's in the back." The crewman pulled him to his feet and Jack draped an arm around him as the man helped him toward the boat. He glanced over his shoulder to see two more in the back of the truck lifting Sweets out as the Marines continued to fire along with the Vipers overhead. Jack reached the side of the boat and was helped inside, the crew careful to avoid any contact with his neck. He lay down on his stomach beside the wounded Marine, already being worked on by a medic.

"You okay, buddy?" asked the Marine, and Jack jerked a thumb at his neck.

"I'm sure I'll be the last to know."

The medic working on the Marine leaned over and took a look. "You'll live, but don't try to pull any of that out or it might change your diagnosis."

"Lovely."

The boat shook and Sweets' body was laid down beside Jack, there little room for ceremony here. The engine roared and they pulled from the shore as Jack reached out and adjusted the blanket so that it fully covered the hero's head. He draped his arm over Sweets' back then closed his eyes, exhausted.

You'll be home soon, my friend.

Outside the Sewage Treatment Plant

Yangon, Myanmar

Red continued forward, firing disciplined rounds as their ammo was running low. The first transport was decimated, those that had managed to get out of the back dead or dying. The second was another story. Protected by the first vehicle, the troops it carried had managed to disembark and spread out.

He glanced over his shoulder at Jagger. "Do we have any rounds for the eighty left?"

"One."

"Now's as good a time as any, don't you think?"

Jagger smiled and swapped out his M4 for the recoilless rifle then took a knee. He aimed then fired from the far right of the road, giving him an angle on the second transport. The 84-millimeter round slammed into the engine compartment and exploded, sending shrapnel in all directions, taking out at least half of those using the truck as cover.

Screams erupted as Red and Mickey continued forward, rounding the lead transport and eliminating any of the remaining survivors.

Red swept the area then signaled for the group to advance. He pointed at Mickey and Jagger. "Cover this flank." He tentatively stepped through the gates, blown apart by one of the airstrikes, hugging the crumbling wall, his weapon quickly sweeping from left to right, searching for any threats. He advanced toward the main entrance, encountering no resistance. The Marines and flight crew spread out to his left and right as the rest of his team covered their sixes, the civilians now within the treatment plant's walls.

He activated his comms. "Control, Zero-Two. We're inside the perimeter. No resistance so far. Where are we heading, over?"

"We fed the plans to your tactical computers with a traced-out route for when you get inside. But for now, just get through those main doors."

Red rushed up the steps to the front doors. He pulled on one and found it locked, then tried the others, finding them the same. People didn't lock up when they were fleeing. They locked themselves inside to keep those they feared out. It meant they could encounter resistance or merely a bunch of plant workers terrified about what was going on outside. The glass was reinforced with wire mesh, so he didn't bother breaking through.

He stepped back and hailed Casey, pointing at the doors. "Blow it."

Casey rushed forward and fit a small charge in place as Red stepped back. "Fire in the hole!" warned Casey, and a small explosion followed. The doors swung open and Red rushed inside the lobby. Several people cried out in fear but he couldn't see them. There was a reception counter to the left where they were likely hiding. He indicated for Casey to take the far end as he advanced. They both rounded the counter at the same time and Red flicked his rifle butt up at the three women cowering in fear.

"On your feet. Hands where I can see them." He had no idea if they understood a word he was saying but his meaning was clear, and all three of them rose, thrusting their hands high. "Anybody speak English?"

Two of them nodded.

"We don't want to hurt anybody. We're just passing through. Do you have any guards here? Anybody with guns?"

The two women shook their heads. "Nobody," said one of them.

Red leaned closer, the muzzle of his rifle aimed directly at the woman's chest. "If you're lying to me, now's your chance to correct that mistake."

She shook her head again. "Not lying, I swear, not lying. Soldiers at entrance left when the shooting started."

Red eased off and jerked his weapon toward the doors. "Get out. Go home."

The three women grabbed their purses from under the counter and awkwardly hurried toward the door, their heels ridiculously high, the males in charge here no doubt setting a dress code for their entertainment, not their female employees' comfort.

"Everybody inside!" shouted Red, those holding at the door surging through. He flipped open the flap protecting his tactical computer and brought up the map, orienting himself, then pointed at a nearby door.

"Let's go, people. It's not going to take them long to figure out where we went."

He pushed through the inner doors and raced down the long corridor revealed, the map indicating there should be stairs at the far end that led to their salvation below ground. He just prayed the plans were accurate and that the women at the front desk hadn't been lying.

He didn't want another death on his hands.

Sewage Outflow Pipe

Yangon, Myanmar

Dawson made certain his ear protection was in place then glanced back at Aynslee who was holding her phone up, recording the proceedings. "Ms. Kai, if you intend to ever hear what you're broadcasting again, you'll put the phone down and cover your ears. This is going to be louder than anything you've ever experienced."

She was well back from where the explosives had been set, farther back than the rest of them.

"Just cup your hands over your ears. Don't plug them, you'll just create pressure. Everyone set?"

Aynslee's phone disappeared into a pocket, her hands covering her ears, and she nodded along with the rest of the team.

Dawson gave the signal to Niner.

"Fire in the hole!" Niner flipped open the cover on the remote detonator then activated the trigger. A series of rapid, nearly simultaneous explosions deafened them as the stress points for the gate blocking their way were targeted. "Stand by!" warned Niner as he made the detonator safe. He rose and rushed forward, checking to make sure all the explosives had detonated. "All clear!" He pushed on the grate, still in place, and cursed. "I would've thought that would take it out."

Atlas stepped forward and shoved Niner aside. "Out of the way, little man. This requires some beef." He shoulder-checked the grate and it fell forward, rattling to a standstill on the pipe.

Dawson smiled. "I knew there was a reason I wanted you on my team."

Atlas flexed, kissing both biceps and Niner rushed forward, duck lips extended. "Can I kiss the muscles that made it happen?"

Atlas extended an arm and grabbed Niner's face with the palm of his hand, holding him back. "Put those things away."

Niner's lips receded and Atlas let him go.

Dawson glanced back. "Ms. Kai, are you okay?"

She shook her head, as if to rid it of a rattle. "I think so. My ears are still ringing, but I can hear you. I can't believe how loud that was."

"Welcome to the life of a soldier. Now you know why so many of our vets have hearing problems." Dawson turned to his team. "Niner, you take point. Just because they're preoccupied out front doesn't mean nobody heard that."

Niner took the lead. "Why am I always on point? Is it because I'm Asian?"

Atlas grunted. "No, it's because you're the tiniest little snowflake here, so you're the least likely to get hit if you stumble upon the enemy."

Niner gave his friend a look. "So, what you're telling me is that you should never be on point?"

"From your lips to BD's ears."

Dawson chuckled. "Let's get going. No time to waste. Red might need some help and I don't want it delayed by you two flirting."

Both Niner and Atlas' heads whipped around toward him. "Flirting?"

Aynslee snickered. "God, I wish I could broadcast this. You guys are priceless."

Dawson smiled at her. "It keeps us sane, ma'am. But don't you worry, when it's needed, we're all dead serious."

Moore/James Residence, Abbotts Park Apartments

Fayetteville, North Carolina

Maggie sat on the couch, clasping her face in horror as everyone watched the live coverage of what was happening in Myanmar. A correspondent embedded with the USS Ronald Reagan was reporting from the flight deck as a helicopter landed behind him and two stretchers were offloaded. The first man was rushed away with an IV carried by one of the crew as he lay prone on the stretcher, his face hidden, bandages visible on his neck. The other was brought out more carefully, with reverence, a colorful blanket draped over him. One of the crewmen stumbled and the stretcher tipped, an arm falling loose, and Maggie gasped at the tattoo revealed, a tattoo she'd recognize anywhere.

"What is it?" asked Vanessa.

"Just shocked that somebody's dead."

Almost everyone was there now, including women that hadn't been read-in, Dawson and the others recognized on the news broadcast resulting in text messages and phone calls going out. Questions were asked that those in the know couldn't answer, like why were their boyfriends in the middle of a warzone when they were supposed to be on a logistics exercise?

She excused herself and headed to the bathroom. She dialed the colonel and he answered immediately.

"Clancy."

"Sir, it's Maggie." Her voice cracked. "I just saw…"

"What did you see?" His voice was gentle, as if he already knew the answer but needed her to say the words.

"Sweets. Is he…"

"Yes, I'm afraid so. Who else knows?"

"I don't think anyone saw the tattoo, but they're going to be replaying that footage over and over. Somebody's going to make the connection and Lisa is on the way."

Clancy muttered a curse. "When do you expect her?"

"Any minute now."

A heavy sigh created a burst of static. "All right. I'll collect the chaplain and base services. Where are you?"

"Vanessa's. They've got no kids, thank God."

"Please tell me she's not pregnant."

"Not that I know of."

"Well, let's hope, because I know they've been trying."

She sniffed. "You know?"

"Ms. Harris, I know everything about those under my command. I'll be there as soon as I can. For God's sake, make sure she doesn't see that television screen. She deserves to hear what happened from his commanding officer, not some damn news report."

"Yes, sir." The doorbell rang and she closed her eyes. "I think she's here, sir."

"Very well. I'm on my way."

The call ended and Maggie yanked a tissue from the box on the back of the toilet and blew her nose then checked her eyes in the mirror. They were puffy, but so were a lot of the eyes here today as everyone worried about the men they loved. She heard Lisa's voice, confirming what she had suspected, and she gasped as she lost the battle to keep her emotions in check. This poor woman was here to be among friends to support each other emotionally through this rare occasion where they knew what they had always suspected, that their men were fighting for their lives with an enemy hell-bent on killing every last one of them. But no one ever came to one of these gatherings thinking it would be *their* loved one that wouldn't be coming home.

You always assumed you were there to comfort the partner of someone else who was lost.

Someone knocked on the door to the bathroom, and she flinched.

"Maggie, are you all right? Lisa is here."

It was Vanessa. Maggie gripped the edges of the vanity, squeezing her eyes shut. "Yes, I'm all right. I'll be out in a minute."

She stared at herself in the mirror.

Please, God, give me the strength to get through this for Lisa's sake.

Sewage Treatment Plant

Yangon, Myanmar

Red hurried down the steps, the stairwell exactly where Langley's plans indicated. They wound down six flights before they reached sub-level 3. So far, they had encountered no resistance, the women working the counter apparently telling the truth. He pulled open one of the double doors then peered inside. He spotted several workers manning their stations, the emergency lighting of the stairwell replaced by a fully lit operations center, obviously on a generator.

He went unnoticed as he quickly assessed the room then stepped back, turning to his team. "Bravo Team, up front."

Those covering their sixes squeezed forward.

"I count eight inside, all civilians, though there could be more. Let's try not to kill anyone unless it's absolutely necessary, but if you need to kneecap somebody, then go ahead. We don't have time for long drawn-out hand-to-hand. As soon as the room is secure, Casey, blow anything between us and that outflow pipe. Just make sure you warn BD's team before you do it. We wouldn't want to damage any of Niner's delicate features."

Snickers responded then Red yanked open the door, rushing inside. "United States Military! Everyone get your hands up!" He broke right as the rest of the team poured in behind him. He fired a single round in the air and made a beeline for the center of the room where a man with gray hair stood, his bearing suggesting he was in charge. "Do you speak English?"

"Yes. I attended Princeton."

"Excellent. We're just passing through." Red pointed at a gangway on the other side of a glass wall, the entrance to three large pipes visible. "Can you confirm those are the outflow pipes?"

"Yes." The man's eyes narrowed. "Are you the Americans from the embassy?"

Red ignored the question. "Can you confirm that the pipe on the left leads to the Yangon River?"

"It does." The man indicated the group from the embassy. "Is *she* one of them?"

"No. These people have nothing to do with what happened with the little girl." Red took the man by the arm, leading him toward the door. "Get us to that pipe and we'll let you go."

The man yanked his arm free. "I won't help you. The American killed a little girl and half her family, and you're helping her escape justice. Even if I didn't support my government, I wouldn't help you."

Red rolled his eyes. "You shouldn't believe your government's propaganda. What you've been told is a lie, but if you won't help, I can respect that." He slung his M4 then grabbed the man around the neck, putting him in a sleeper hold. "Mickey, check that door."

Mickey rushed over to a door beside the glass wall and yanked it open. He poked his head inside then gave a thumbs-up. "Clear path to our exit point." He scrunched his nose. "Lovely smell too. If this is sewage treatment, they're doing it wrong."

A woman raised her hand. "It's on bypass because of the power failure."

Red smiled at her. "I'm sure you do a fantastic job on a normal day." He pointed at the door, indicating for everyone to head through. He lowered the unconscious body gently to the floor then headed after the others. He turned to the remaining workers. "Your boss will be fine in a few minutes, he's just unconscious. Don't follow us, and I highly recommend you don't go outside. It's too dangerous. Just wait here for your people to find you." He tapped the doorframe as he stepped through. "And I'll be rigging this to explode if anyone opens it, so don't try to follow us."

He closed the door and spotted several of the workers rushing toward their boss. He made a show of manipulating the lock as he counted to ten, then followed the others through the outflow pipe, raw sewage sloshing at his feet.

The things I do for my country.

CHARLIE FOXTROT

Sewage Outflow Pipe

Yangon, Myanmar

Dawson sprinted forward and came to a halt when Niner raised a fist. Lights bouncing ahead indicated somebody was coming.

"Thunderbolt!" called Niner.

"Lightning!" responded the familiar voice of Red.

"Very, very frightening me!" sang Niner.

Atlas smacked him on the back, sending him tumbling forward. "If I hear Bohemian Rhapsody again, I'm breaking necks."

Dawson stepped forward as Red came into sight.

"My God, you have no idea how happy I am to see you guys," exclaimed his friend.

Dawson smiled. "Same here." He put a hand on his best friend's shoulder. "How are you feeling?"

Red frowned. "Better than Sweets."

Dawson clenched his jaw. "We'll mourn our brother when we're out of here. But you're a hundred percent?"

Red shrugged. "I'd say more like ninety, but don't worry, I won't hold you up. Sweets died saving my ass. There's no way in hell I'm letting that go to waste."

"I hear you, brother." Dawson turned his attention to the ragtag group. "Any injuries?"

"One minor, but she's stable. Everyone's just exhausted."

"I guess so. There's a reason hockey players do forty-five-second shifts. You guys have been on the ice for the whole game."

Niner turned. "Did someone say ice? If anyone's holding out, hand some over. My chestnuts are roasting."

Atlas grunted. "Forget his chestnuts, my coco de mers are about to catch fire."

Niner eyed him. "What the hell is a coco de mer?"

Atlas grinned. "It's the biggest nut in the world. Up to fifty pounds each."

Spock cocked an eyebrow. "I think the two of you are the biggest nuts in the world."

Dawson activated his comms. "Control, Zero-One. We've met up with Zero-Two's team. Heading for the river now, over."

"Copy that, Zero-One. Be advised that hostiles have made entry into the plant. It looks like they know where you went. It's only a matter of time before they figure out why, over."

"Copy that, Control. Can you confirm that you've had eyes on the outflow pipe the entire time?"

"Affirmative, Zero-One. We've had eyes on the pipe the entire time you've been inside and nobody has followed, over."

"Copy that, Control. We're heading out now. Zero-One, out." Dawson turned to the others. "Okay, let's go! We're going to have enemy soldiers on our asses any minute now, and we've got no place to hide. Niner and Atlas, Control's confirmed the way is clear ahead so let's make the best speed possible. Just warn us of anything in the water that might cause injury."

"Yes, Sergeant Major," replied Niner, sprinting ahead, Atlas on his heels.

Dawson turned to the others. "Let's go! As fast as you can. Shout out if you encounter something that might hurt the person behind you."

Moore/James Residence, Abbotts Park Apartments
Fayetteville, North Carolina

Maggie sat on the couch, her eyes glued to the screen, the loop showing Sweets' tattoo already having played three times since his wife arrived, and each time she had managed to distract the woman. But one of these times she would fail.

The doorbell rang and Maggie sprang to her feet, waving Vanessa off from answering the door to her own apartment. "I'll get it."

Vanessa eyed her but didn't protest. "All right."

Maggie rushed down the hall and opened the door, sucking in an involuntary breath at the sight of Colonel Clancy in full dress uniform, accompanied by one of the base chaplains and a woman she recognized from family services who would guide Lisa through the horrendous journey ahead.

"Ms. Harris. Is she here?"

"Yes, sir."

Somebody gasped behind her and she spun to see Vanessa standing there, her eyes welling with tears.

Maggie shook her head. "Not you."

Vanessa's shoulders slumped in relief and she gripped her temples with her thumb and forefinger as the tears escaped. "Who?" she asked, her voice barely a murmur.

"Lisa."

"Did somebody say my name?" asked Lisa as she rounded the corner then froze, her jaw dropping at the sight of Clancy and who was with him. She backed away. "No. Please, no."

"I'm so sorry," said Maggie, her voice cracking.

Lisa collapsed and screamed, the anguished wail shattering Maggie's heart. She and Vanessa rushed toward their friend. Maggie dropped to her knees and wrapped her arms around the sobbing woman.

Lisa stared at her. "You knew, didn't you? That was why you kept trying to distract me."

"I'm so sorry. I just found out a few minutes ago."

"How could you do that to me? How could you not tell me?"

Clancy stepped forward. "I'm afraid that's my doing, ma'am. I asked Ms. Harris not to tell you so that I could tell you in person." He took a knee beside her. "Mrs. Peters, I regret to inform you that your husband, Sergeant Donald Peters, was killed today in a training accident." He held up a hand to everyone about to protest, the rest of the guests now crammed in the hallway. "You and I both know that's bullshit. You saw on television what's happening. You should know that your husband died a hero. He remained behind with one of his fallen comrades, singlehandedly fought off the enemy, then successfully resuscitated his comrade, who is now alive and well because of your husband's efforts. During the attempt to reunite with the rest of the team, your husband was killed. Extreme efforts were undertaken to recover his body so that he could receive an honorable burial on home soil, and those efforts were successful. You should know that I'm nominating him for a Silver Star." He placed a hand on the trembling woman's shoulder. "You should be extremely proud of your husband, but please remember that you're still bound by your non-disclosure agreement. This mission is classified. Even if the networks are covering it, no one can know how your husband truly died. But rest assured those in the know, and a grateful nation, mourn with you."

He extended a hand and Lisa took it. He helped her to her feet and she squared her shoulders as Vanessa handed her a tissue. "Thank you, Colonel, for coming to inform me personally. I know you didn't have to do that and I don't want to keep you from your duties since the rest of the team is still out there."

Clancy smiled at her and patted her arm. "You're a brave woman, Mrs. Peters, and it has not only been my privilege to know your husband, but to know you as well, and never forget, you'll always be part of the Unit. I brought the Chaplain and a Family Services rep to help you through this difficult time. If you ever need anything, you just let me know."

Lisa sniffed hard. "Thank you, Colonel." She reached out and took Maggie's hand, squeezing it. "There is one thing you can do for me."

"Name it."

"We were planning Maggie's wedding. We wanted to do it as soon as they returned from the mission. I don't want my husband's death to stop that."

Maggie gasped and squeezed Lisa's hand. "Oh, God, no, we can't do it now. We'll wait. It's all right."

Lisa firmly shook her head. "No, this is exactly what we were talking about. Something's always interrupting your plans. You two deserve to get married, and he wouldn't want his death delaying that any further. Consider it our wedding gift to you."

Maggie hugged Lisa hard, the two women sobbing in each other's arms. Clancy said his farewells then left as the rest of those gathered shuffled forward, a large group hug soon underway. Maggie closed her eyes as she was squeezed from all sides. She would be married soon, but the day would be bittersweet. Part of her didn't want to have the wedding now, to wait until everyone had had time to sufficiently mourn Sweets' death, but that would dishonor Lisa's generous wish.

Then an idea occurred to her of how they could have their day and celebrate not only their nuptials but Sweets' life.

And she smiled.

Operations Center 3, CIA Headquarters

Langley, Virginia

Leroux stood behind his station in the operations center, his hands on his hips, mimicking his boss, Morrison, who stood beside him. He couldn't believe they had made it this far. A Marine gunny sergeant was dead and so was Sweets, but as of this moment, all of the civilians were alive, half of them safely aboard the USS Ronald Reagan. Jack was safe and would soon be on his feet after the glass shards had been removed from his neck, and he was already demanding to be sent back into the fight. The only thing stopping him was Leroux's request that he remain with Sweets until relieved by one of his brothers-in-arms. That had silenced Jack's protests, at least for now, though he had been given a secure tablet so he could monitor the goings on.

Tong indicated the tactical display. "They're starting to spread out a little too much."

He shifted his attention from enemy troop movements to the zoomed-in display showing the locator beacons of Bravo Team, the distance between the two farthest points indicating the spread was now approaching one hundred yards. Something was slowing them up, and that wouldn't do. Once Wings was signaled, he'd have the boat in position in less than a minute and they would have little time to load all those people on board before somebody noticed.

He activated his comms. "Zero-One, Control. You guys are spreading out too far. It's going to take too long to load. Recommend you tighten up the line before signaling One-Two, over."

"Acknowledged, Control. We've got some twisted ankles down here and there's a lot of debris in the water. Zero-One, out."

Morrison pointed at a satellite image on the right-hand side of the display. "What the hell is that?"

Leroux peered at the screen. Three boats in a cluster were heading into the mouth of the river. "Zoom in on those."

Tong tapped at her keyboard, isolating a shot of the three vessels. She enlarged the feed to fill half the display, the computer automatically analyzing the targets then comparing the wire outlines to their database, the names and general specs appearing beside each in bubbles. "Looks like three navy vessels. Coincidence?"

Morrison dismissed the notion. "I don't believe in coincidence, but even if it is, depending on which direction they head, they're going to be encountering our people at the exact same time as they're coming out of that pipe."

"What do we do?" asked Child. "Keep them in the pipe until they go past?"

"No, they're fish in a barrel in there." Leroux pointed at the display. "Sonya, get those targets to the Ronald Reagan, priority fire mission."

"I'm on it."

Leroux activated his comms. "Zero-One, Control. You have three enemy vessels heading upriver now. ETA your position in less than five minutes, over."

"Copy that, Control. Request you do something about it. There's no way we're taking out three naval vessels with M4s, over."

"Airstrike has been called in, Zero-One."

"ETA?"

Leroux glanced at Tong who held up four fingers. "Four minutes, over."

"Copy that, Control. Zero-One, out."

Morrison frowned as he stared at the tactical display. "Definitely a Charlie Foxtrot."

Leroux agreed. A tragic traffic accident should have ended with the death of the little girl, followed by reports filed, compensation paid to the family along with sincere apologies for what had happened. Louise Chambers leaving the vehicle had escalated the situation far beyond anything anyone could have imagined. Equally shocking, however, was the reaction of the Myanmar military. Why had they opened fire with RPGs on the rescue helicopters? They had to know what the response would be. It had him thinking there was some rogue element involved, but that would be for the analysts to figure out later.

For now, his focus was turning this Charlie Foxtrot into an ultimately successful rescue mission. What was currently a disaster could one day be taught as an example of how Navy, Air Force, Army, and intelligence assets working together could turn what appeared to be a mission failure into a mission success.

Morrison regarded him. "Penny for your thoughts."

Leroux chuckled. "Sorry, sir. I was just thinking how this Charlie Foxtrot has a chance of turning into a success."

"From your lips to God's ears, son." Morrison gestured at the display. "Let's just pray that what's about to happen doesn't end up cementing this mission as a complete failure. There's just too much that can still go wrong."

Wunna Residence

Yangon, Myanmar

Eindra came to a stop in front of the gate and pressed the buzzer. Much to her surprise, it sounded despite the entire city still being blacked out. She peered through the gate to see several lights on at the house, and she finally noticed the roar of a generator from behind the walls.

"Yes?" asked a voice over the speaker.

"I'm Eindra. I'm the daughter of Yeshe. He's injured. I need help."

"Come up to the house."

A buzzer sounded and she pushed on the gate then maneuvered her scooter through and closed the gate behind her. She gave her bike some gas, allowing her to regain her balance as she picked up speed. She reached the front entrance of the home, far grander than hers, though nothing compared to what most leaders of the junta enjoyed.

Her father's friend, Wunna, rushed down the steps, his jaw dropping at the sight of her father. "My word! What's happened?"

"He was hit in the head with the butt of a rifle by a soldier. I took him to the hospital and they said to keep him awake and to bring him back if he got worse, but then the soldiers came looking for us. I think he's getting worse but I can't bring him back. They'll arrest us and they'll beat him. He'll die for sure!"

"Let's get him inside." Wunna helped her groggy father off the scooter then they both carried him inside the house.

Wunna's wife gasped. "Oh no, what's happened?"

"He's been hit in the head." They lay him down on the couch and her father groaned, reaching for her. She dropped by his side, taking his outstretched hand.

"Yes, Father, I'm here. You're safe, we're both safe. We're at Wunna's house."

Wunna smiled down at her father. "Hello, old friend, you're safe here, and so is your daughter, but we have to figure out what's wrong with you."

Wunna's son raced into the room. "Father, they just—" He froze, noticing their guests.

Wunna indicated him. "You remember my son, Thuza?"

Eindra nodded. "Of course."

"Thuza, do you remember Yeshe and his daughter, Eindra?"

Thuza's head rapidly bobbed., the young boy staring with teenage awkwardness at her. "Father?"

"What is it? You had something to say?"

"You had me writing down names, and when I heard her on the gate speaker, I thought they sounded familiar so I checked. They're after them. Her and her father. They know they're headed this way."

Wunna's eyes narrowed. "They know they're coming here specifically?"

"No, sir, they know they were spotted heading south from the hospital. They've been named priority targets. They've ordered all units to be on the lookout. It's only a matter of time before they start searching. And father..." Thuza hesitated.

"Out with it, there's no time to waste."

"Father, the order was given by someone named Captain Champo. I checked your list. He wears the red scarf."

Eindra tensed at Wunna's reaction. "This is far more serious than I thought. At first, I assumed your father had been hit by a random soldier for no reason. But they're after you both specifically. If the Red Scarves catch you, you'll never be seen again. Why are they after you?" He raised a hand, cutting off her response. "No, I don't want to know. It has something to do with what's going on in the city though, doesn't it?"

"Yes, sir. What are we going to do?"

Wunna scratched his chin. "I'm not sure, but you can't stay here for long. The phones are down. We have electricity because of the generator, but we can't communicate with anybody."

A long slow sigh escaped from her father and she returned her attention to him then cried out. She dropped back to her knees and placed her hand on his face. "Father, can you hear me? Father?"

A tear rolled down his cheek and his mouth opened. She leaned in. "Forgive me, precious flower." His head slumped to the side and his chest stopped moving. A hand roughly shoved her aside and Wunna began chest compressions as tears flowed down her cheeks. She clasped her hands to her face and prayed like she never had before, begging for her father's life, her prayers to go unanswered.

She was alone.

Sewage Outflow Pipe
Yangon, Myanmar

Dawson could see the light ahead, Niner and Atlas already at the opening. He should be signaling Wings by now to bring the boat, but they were too spread out. The civilians were exhausted and most didn't have proper footwear to be slogging through the uncertain waters of a sewage outflow pipe.

A shot rang out behind them followed by a shout. He cursed. The enemy in pursuit had caught up. The rapid fire of M4s on full-auto replied and several of the civilians screamed in terror.

"Keep moving! Keep moving!" he shouted before activating his comms. "One-Two, Zero-One. Bring the boat now, over."

"Roger that, Zero-One. Moving into position now. ETA sixty seconds, over."

"Acknowledged, One-Two. Be advised, we are taking fire from the rear."

"Understood, Zero-One. We'll make this as efficient as possible. One-Two, out."

Niner turned. "BD, we've got troubles here!"

Dawson rushed toward the entrance as Niner and Atlas opened fire as the naval vessels Leroux had advised them about arrived. "Control, Zero-One, where the hell's that airstrike? I've got hostiles at both ends of the pipe." He reached the entrance and dropped to a knee, opening fire on the lead vessel, its lone armament a deck mounted .50 cal. "Keep that fifty out of commission," he ordered Niner and Atlas who had already downed the gunner and kept the replacements at bay. He opened fire on the pilot house, his armor-piercing rounds making quick work of it, the thin sheeting providing those inside with little protection.

The boat veered to the right, away from them, and they switched their attention to the next boat. Its .50 opened up on them, forcing them to fall back as the enemy gunfire tore apart the entrance of the drainage pipe. Gunfire continued from the rear, and Dawson hustled past the crouching civilians, the Marines and aircrew once again using their bodies as human shields. Muzzle flashes from ahead revealed the enemy, less than one hundred yards away.

He dropped beside Red. "Sitrep!"

"The situation sucks! We're sitting ducks here. Once they get organized, Sweets is going to have a lot of company."

Dawson frowned. "It's not much better looking at the other end, but here we've got options." He grabbed a cloth bag as it drifted by then handed it to Jimmy. "Everybody hand their C4 down! Anything that goes boom!"

The bag was passed down the line, everyone dropping in whatever they had left, and it was soon returned. Dawson jammed a detonator into one of the chunks of plastic explosives then tied a knot in the top of the bag. "Suppression fire!"

Four guns opened up on full-auto and Dawson rose to a knee, whipping his makeshift bomb as far as he could. It splashed in the water far enough ahead he was satisfied they would be safe.

"Fire in the hole!" he warned and triggered the device with a flick of his finger on the remote detonator. The explosion was massive and shouts of terror and pain grew behind him as the unprepared civilians reacted. The enormous explosion, far larger than he had intended, tore apart the tunnel behind them, and he dropped into the sewage as a wave of flame, debris, and water raced toward them.

Maybe I overdid it a little.

Yangon River

Yangon, Myanmar

"Holy shit!" exclaimed Roy from behind the wheel of their boat as Wings lay prone on the prow, firing at the lead vessel pouring lead at the opening of the pipe his friends were trapped in. A massive surge of water and flame erupted from the pipe and Wings spotted at least three bodies flying into the river along with debris ejected by whatever had just happened inside. It had to be a detonation, and he prayed it was triggered by a team member and not the enemy.

He continued to fire on the vessel, unable to silence the .50 cal until this point, when it fell silent on its own, the gunner standing tall to get a look at what had just happened. Spock put two in the man's chest then fired at the two replacements rushing forward, dropping them to the deck.

He pointed to starboard. "We've got people in the water!"

"I see them," replied Roy, the cameraman having grown up on the water piloting his father's shrimping boat for years until it was lost during

Katrina. Wings had yielded the position when he had discovered this, figuring a qualified person on the rifle could prove more valuable.

He activated his comms. "Control, where the hell's that airstrike?"

"Duck," was the reply, and Wings grinned as four F-18s ripped by overhead and moments later the three boats erupted in flames, their weapons silenced, their crews dead, leaving Wings with a difficult job ahead.

Sewage Outflow Pipe

Yangon, Myanmar

Dawson pushed up out of the sewage and peered back at his handiwork. There was no gunfire coming from the enemy position anymore, and he risked shining a light down the pipe and found a wall of dirt where there had once been a steel pipe tall enough for a man to walk through upright.

"Is everybody all right?" he asked.

Red groaned. "It's bad enough when the enemy is trying to kill me, but my best friend? What the hell were you thinking?"

Dawson shrugged. "I figured I had one shot at it, so better make it a good one. It was bigger than I expected, however." He cocked an ear. "Is it just me or is there no more gunfire from the front either?"

"Right now, I'm just amazed I'm hearing you."

Dawson rose. "Niner, report." He spotted a hand wave from the end of the pipe.

"I'm alive, no thanks to you. Atlas, did you crack your mega nuts?"

ADER KENNEDY

Atlas' deep voice boomed. "I don't know, but if I can't have children, I'm sending Vanessa after BD."

"Bravo Team, sound off then check the civilians." He activated his comms. "One-Two, Zero-One, report, over."

"This is One-Two. I've got people in the water here."

Dawson cursed as the count-off held at five.

"We're missing two civilians," shouted one of the flight crew.

"The Marines are gone too," reported Jimmy. "And Mickey is missing."

"One-Two, we're missing at least five. What's your count, over?"

"I've got eyes on four, but there's a lot of debris."

"Where's Aynslee?" asked Niner.

Dawson spun quickly, surveying the area. "Ms. Kai, are you with us?" There was no answer. He cursed, reactivating his comms. "One-Two, we're missing our CNN reporter, as well. Make that at least six missing."

"Copy that, Zero-One. Suggest you get on board and help with recovery operations ASAP, over."

"Roger that, we're coming to the hole." Dawson turned to the others. "Get everyone up and out and onto the boat. No hesitations. Red and Jimmy, sweep the water as you move forward. Make sure there's nobody under it. I don't want to get on board and find out we left somebody behind that we can't come back for."

"We're on it, BD," replied Red as he and Jimmy spread out, kicking at the water as everyone else rose. Dawson turned to see the prow of the boat appear. Niner caught a line tossed to him and handed it to Atlas who single-handedly pulled the boat into position before tying it off.

"Let's go, let's go, let's go!" shouted Wings from outside. Niner and Atlas leaped aboard and the flight crew assisted the remaining civilians as Dawson stripped out of his gear. He pointed at Spock and Jagger.

"You two stay geared up with Red and Jimmy, the rest of you out of your gear. We're going in the river." He removed the last of his heavy equipment then stepped past those still queuing to get on the boat. He tossed his gear and his weapon onto the deck then jumped on board and headed for the prow. He spotted a body in the water and dove in. He swam with the current and quickly caught up, flipping the body over. It was a Marine corporal. Dawson punched him in the gut and the man gasped, water bursting out of his mouth. "You okay?"

The Marine momentarily panicked before he oriented himself. "Holy shit, what the hell just happened?"

"You'll read it in the report if you ever get to see it. Can you swim?"

"I'm not sure."

"Can you float?"

"Yeah, I can do that."

"Okay. Just try to float back to America. We'll pick you up on the way."

The Marine gave a thumbs-up. "I'll try my best."

Dawson tread water and spotted another body just ahead. Behind him, other team members were diving in. He glanced back to see Niner and Atlas had most of the ragtag group on board and they would soon be casting off. He had somehow misjudged that explosion. It shouldn't have been that big, not with that much C4, but that didn't matter right now. He had to save these people, because if he didn't, he would have been the single biggest cause of death on this entire damn mission.

He swam hard toward a woman struggling to stay above the surface. He reached her and wrapped his arm around her from behind so that she couldn't grab at him with her arms. "Calm down, I've got you. You're going to be all right."

She continued to flail then slowly settled. "Oh, thank God. I can't swim."

"Lucky for you, ma'am, I can. Now, just relax. You're going to be all right." Two toots of a foghorn behind him had him glancing to see the boat had cast off from the pipe and was now heading downriver. "The boat's coming," he reassured the woman as he looked about to do a head count. He spotted a few of his team in the water that appeared to have rescued people. He leaned back and gently kicked, slowing their pace. "I've got one civilian female alive. Marine, are you still with us?"

"Yes, Sergeant Major!"

"Good to hear. Bravo Team, report!"

"I've got the second Marine alive!" shouted Casey. "And I've got Mickey! He's unconscious but alive."

"I've got our other missing civilian," called Atlas from the boat.

"Anybody have our reporter?" Dawson waited and nobody answered. He cursed. "Keep your eyes out for her. We'll never hear the end of it if we lose her." He activated his comms. "Control, Zero-One. We appear to have lost Aynslee Kai. I repeat, we might have lost Aynslee Kai."

Heading South

Yangon, Myanmar

Eindra raced toward the river on Wunna's son's scooter, the dark blue distinctly different from the bright red of her own, the description having gone out on the radio that Wunna was monitoring as part of the opposition's resistance to military rule. Her father was dead and her mother had died giving birth to her. She had nobody. Her father was her world.

And now the military was after her.

Wunna had a satellite phone that he used to communicate with exiled opposition members around the world—anything over regular lines could be monitored. It was useless for communicating with anyone within the city since all mobile networks and landlines were down, but there was one call it could make, and that was to Jack, the man who owed her family a favor for helping the Americans. She had called the number and left a message explaining who she was, what was happening, and where she intended to head, then begged whoever got the message to help.

She had to leave the country. There was no place for her now in Myanmar. The Red Scarves were after her and that was a death sentence, though that death would be a long time coming. She would be tortured and raped for weeks or months, perhaps even years, potentially sold into the sex trade.

She had to reach the mouth of the river where Wunna said the reports suggested the Americans were heading. If someone spotted her there, they could take her with them, but they would only do so if Jack told them to. She spotted a roadblock ahead and braked hard, guiding her scooter into an alleyway to avoid it. Somebody shouted and a gunshot rang out, and she soiled herself a little.

She was dying long before any help could arrive.

Yangon, Myanmar

Dawson climbed aboard after handing the woman up to Atlas. He rose to his feet and turned to Red. "Status?"

"Everyone's alive and accounted for except for Ms. Kai. We're watching the water and the shoreline, but nothing so far. I've got Wings taking us full throttle out of here."

Dawson agreed with the decision. "Good. We can't put all these lives at risk for one civilian who shouldn't have been here in the first place." He turned to her cameraman, Roy. "We've got eyes in the sky looking for her and if we find her, we'll try to get her out. But I can't make any promises. She was never part of this mission, and, unfortunately, she might have been killed from that damned blast for all we know."

Niner cleared his throat. "Um, BD, about that, I think it's my fault."

"What do you mean?"

"Well, when you asked us to hand up our explosives, I didn't realize what you were using it for until it was too late. I handed you a shitload of thermite. I should have asked first. That blast was way more than you were planning for because of me."

It was a screw-up, a major one, but it wasn't just Niner's screw-up. It was his own. He should have checked everything handed forward, but in the heat of the moment and the dark, he had made an assumption, an assumption that might have got a woman killed. "I asked for explosives to be handed forward and wasn't specific. It was my fault." Several of the men gave him a look but said nothing, realizing what he was doing. He was covering Niner's ass. Niner bowed his head slightly, acknowledging silently what had just been done for him, then Dawson carried on. "We're not out of this yet, people. I want everybody as flat on the deck as possible, away from prying eyes. The Burmese are going to be putting everything they can on us. They know we're here and they know where we're going."

USS Ronald Reagan

Bay of Bengal

Jack's CIA-customized Casio watch sent an electrical pulse through his wrist, indicating he had a secure message. He glanced over his shoulder at the rather attractive nurse working on him. "How's it looking?"

"You'll be fine. I got the last of the glass out. It looked worse than it was. The bleeding has stopped. I suggest taking it easy for a few days. Let things heal enough before you return to whatever voodoo it is you do."

He grinned. "I like you."

"You'd like me even better out of this uniform."

Jack turned his head and his grin spread. "I bet I would."

She slapped his shoulder. "I meant a nice dress, dinner and dancing."

"So, did you decide you wanted to go out with me when you heard I was a hero or when you saw how gorgeous I was?"

She shoved his head, facing it forward. "Well, I knew you were a hero, and then I saw you were gorgeous. But then you opened your mouth and I found out you were arrogant."

His shoulders slumped. "Ah, my self-confidence is getting me in trouble again."

She continued working on him. "Not that much trouble. I've got shore leave coming up in a week. I was thinking of taking it in Yokosuka. If someone happened to be there at the same time…"

Jack smiled. "What an odd coincidence. I was planning on taking a little personal time in Yokosuka as well."

She finished taping off a large bandage that covered the back of his neck and shoulders then patted it gently as she rounded the bed to face him. She wrote something on his file then held it up. "If we're going to go on a date, don't you think I should know your name?"

He smiled at her. "Call me Jack."

"Jack what?"

"Just Jack." He hopped off the table. "Now, I have to go back to work."

She frowned. "Hey, you need to take it easy for a few days."

He tapped his watch. "Unfortunately, I don't think that's in the cards."

Yangon Riverbank

Yangon, Myanmar

Aynslee Kai coughed, water bursting from her lungs. Someone shoved her onto her side and pounded on her back as she continued to expel water. She finally drew a deep breath, sending delicious oxygen flooding through her system, and her senses returned. She wasn't sure what had happened. She'd been on her knees, recording what was going on when someone yelled, "Fire in the hole!" She was well back from the explosion but hadn't been prepared for its intensity nor the wall of water that came with it. She remembered being hit, but that was it. She must have been knocked out cold.

She opened her eyes and was surprised to see several locals around her, shirtless men, perhaps fishermen. She sat upright, questions asked of her in Burmese she shook her head to then extended her hands up. She was hauled to her feet and she checked herself over for any injuries, finding nothing beyond minor scrapes and what would eventually be bruising.

She looked about to find she was on the riverbank. She peered upriver but couldn't see the pipe they had come from, though smoke billowing just around a bend would suggest she hadn't gone too far. She turned to the men that had rescued her. "Does anyone speak English?"

"English?" asked one of them.

"Yes. Do you speak English?"

"No English."

She pointed at them then tapped beside her eye. "Americans. Have you seen any Americans?"

One of the men figured out what she was asking, translating for the others, then everyone nodded and pointed downriver. Her heart sank a little. It meant anyone who could help her was nowhere near here. She checked her watch and found it shattered. She tapped it. "How long?" She put her hands together then slowly drew them apart. "How long ago did you see the Americans? How many minutes?"

More discussion then a man held up five fingers and swiveled his wrist, indicating it was an approximation.

She smiled. "Thank you."

She suddenly remembered her satphone and reached for it, but found the pocket she kept it in empty and cursed. No one was coming to her rescue. "Oh no!" She searched herself again, finding her cellphone with all the footage she had taken gone as well. Everything she had done was for naught.

She turned downriver and sprinted as fast as she could along the shore, but there was no way she could catch up. The boat would be moving with the current and had a motor. She was more concerned with the authorities who would be swarming this area at any moment. She had to put as much distance between her and the aftermath of their escape as she could.

If she reached the coast, there was a chance a drone could spot her, as she had no doubt they were searching for her. Even though she had chosen to be there and those men had threatened to leave her behind, after seeing the lengths they had gone to save innocent lives and the sacrifices they had made, she had no doubt they were empty threats designed merely to discourage her and Roy from coming with them. But when push came to shove, she would be treated like any other civilian. They had likely searched for her, but only briefly as it was more important to save everyone else rather than risk those lives in the hopes of finding her alive.

The fishermen behind her shouted at her, but she ignored them, and prayed no one would turn her in. She had an advantage over most of the others. She was Asian with brown skin and could blend with the locals far easier than her ruddy-cheeked cameraman who couldn't get a tan.

Sirens over her right shoulder sent her heart into overdrive. She reached for her press credentials which might save her life and cursed when she found they weren't there. She reached down to find her fanny pack still in place. She didn't carry a purse while on assignment, it was simply too impractical. The fashion faux pas though allowed her to carry everything she needed, and she could feel her passport and other items still inside. The press pass, however, she displayed by law, and had lost it at some point during the day's events.

She spotted the mouth of the river ahead and cried out in frustration as she came to a stop. The river split, or more accurately, two rivers merged, one running along her left down the east side of the city, the other wrapping around the western and southern portions, cutting her off from the far bank that she needed to get to.

She spotted a teenage boy in a small boat preparing to push off. She opened her fanny pack and retrieved a wad of bills, then raced toward him, waving her hands in the air. "Excuse me, do you speak English?"

The boy looked up at her, wide-eyed. "No English."

She held up the bills, splaying them out so that he could see what was likely more money than he'd ever been shown at one time in his life. She tapped her chest and pointed to the far side of the river, then at his boat, then at him. "You take your boat over there." She waved the bills. His eyes bulged again. He looked across the river and jabbed his finger at her then the other side, saying something. She nodded. "Yes, yes. Take me over there. You'll get money."

He grinned and stepped aside. She climbed into the small boat and he pushed it into the water then hopped in after her, working the oars, the current handling most of the effort. She heard something overhead and looked up to see a drone slowly making its way up the river. She raised her hands in the air and waved, praying that not only was it one of their own, but that whoever was monitoring the footage didn't mistake her for a local because of the color of her skin.

Yangon River

Yangon, Myanmar

Wings guided the prow of the boat to the sandy riverbank, bringing them to an abrupt halt. Dawson jumped onto the shore with Niner, Atlas, and Jimmy, then fanned out up the embankment, taking covering positions as everyone else disembarked behind them. Helicopter rotors thundered to their left from the south, and two F-18s screeched past overhead, reminding anyone who might interfere what was in store for them should they choose to do so.

He checked over his shoulder to see the boat almost empty. "Hurry up, people! Our rides are here!"

Gunfire chattered ahead.

"Hold your fire," he ordered. There was no evidence it was aimed at them and it sounded too distant. Returning fire would merely reveal their position that for the moment was hidden by the riverbank being a good ten feet higher than the river.

"All clear!" announced Wings as he hopped to shore.

Dawson rose and grabbed a smoke grenade off his belt. "Pop smoke," he ordered as he pulled the pin and tossed the grenade. Several more canisters flew, and the view between them and the city quickly obscured. It meant they couldn't see the enemy, and the enemy couldn't see them, but it also, more importantly, gave the pilots a clearer view of where they were.

The first Super Huey touched down not one hundred yards away, enemy gunfire instantly increasing. Viper attack helicopters thundered past them, their weapons' pods and cannons opening fire.

Dawson waved at the group. "Let's go, let's go, let's go!" He sprinted toward the first chopper, firing into the smoke as the rest of his team did the same, the flight crew and Marines assisting the civilians. Dawson reached the chopper first, slamming his shoulder into the side, using it as cover as he continued to fire. The first civilian was loaded on board, then another and another. A bullet whipped past him, pinging off the fuselage. He didn't bother ducking—it had already missed, but it meant they were in range.

"Two more!" shouted a crewman from inside. Dawson glanced over his shoulder to see the man pointing. "Everyone else in the other chopper!" The final two were loaded and the door slammed shut as the Super Huey lifted off, Dawson giving the pilot a thumbs-up before continuing his suppression fire. The smoke was temporarily blown away by the rotors as the helicopter banked toward the ocean, revealing scores of the enemy closing in.

Dawson and his team slowly fell back toward the second chopper as the remaining flight crew and Marines climbed in along with several members of his team. The fully laden chopper lifted off, revealing a third chopper behind it, a member of its flight crew leaning out the door, beckoning them to hurry.

Dawson turned to the others. "Let's go, gentlemen, I think we've overstayed our welcome."

"Ya think?" retorted Niner as they rapidly fell back toward their final means of escape. Two Viper helicopters banked hard, coming to an abrupt halt overhead, their weapon systems raining hellfire on the enemy positions, the entire area free of civilians and open season. Niner slapped him on the back, signaling it was his turn to board.

Dawson turned and stepped onto the skid, grabbing the airframe with one hand as he continued to fire on the enemy. "Let's go!" The pilot lifted off and the helicopter banked hard, Dawson hanging out the side as he continued to fire. It leveled out as it rushed toward the nearby ocean and he climbed inside. The crewman slammed the door shut and he took a seat among his men as rounds continued to pelt the reinforced fuselage.

"We're over the water," announced the pilot as they continued to gain speed. "The other choppers are already in international airspace. We will be in a couple of minutes. Did everybody make it out?"

Dawson shook his head, the pilot's jubilant mood wasted on him and his men. "Not everyone."

South of Yangon, Myanmar

Champo roared in frustration as he emptied his mag into the air, the helicopters far out of range. He had expected the Americans to use the same beach they had before, when either the CIA spy or traitor had escaped with the American soldier's body, but they had gone farther south. By the time he had reached the scene reported by his men, the Americans were long gone, and now the group from the embassy were gone too, his chance for revenge stolen from him.

Now no one would pay for what had happened to his niece and brother.

He threw his AK-47 on the ground then kicked it. His fists clenched as he bent over and screamed. He had no way to vent his anger, no way to satisfy the blood lust that consumed him. They had killed two Americans, as far as he was aware—one on the rooftop of the embassy and one outside the electronics shop by his own hand. There was some satisfaction in that, though not much. He wanted to feel flesh, to hear the screams as he sliced the skin off his enemy while his victim was forced to look at pictures of those America had killed.

The Americans were gone but they had been helped. Yeshe and his daughter had lied. That was the only explanation for them leaving for the hospital without telling his men. They had sneaked away and that was a sign of guilt. He had to find them. He had already issued the orders and made it clear that the Red Scarves wanted the father and daughter, and anyone protecting them would be tortured and executed if they didn't turn them over immediately. It was only a matter of time.

No one defied the Red Scarves.

He stood on the road near the shore, staring at the dots on the horizon, each representing a lost opportunity for revenge, and it ate him up inside. A small engine whined behind him and he turned to see what civilian was crazy enough to come into a war zone, the entire area decimated by the American helicopters and planes only minutes ago. He spotted a young woman on a scooter riding through the chaos and rolled his eyes.

Fool.

He turned back to stare at the objects of his hatred, but the helicopters on the horizon were no longer visible. A drone flew past overhead, heading upriver, and his eyes narrowed as he spotted a second drone in the sky, again heading north. If the Americans had all escaped, why were they still sending drones in?

His jaw dropped. They were searching for someone. They had left somebody behind. It could be anyone, a man or woman from the embassy, a soldier. He turned and pointed at the girl on the scooter.

"Stop her! Stop everyone! The Americans are looking for someone and they'll be coming through here to try to reach the ocean. I want a cordon that not even a fly can get through from riverbank to riverbank." He pointed up at the sky. "And let's see if we can shoot some of those damn drones down. They're starting to really piss me off."

Eindra ignored everything going on around her, instead focusing only on what lay directly in front of her tire. She had cut across the south end of the city and a friend of Wunna's had ferried her across the river, but not before she had encountered an unavoidable roadblock. Everyone on a red scooter had been pulled over and searched. She had been waved past on her borrowed blue bike, then made good time.

But she had arrived too late. She had seen the helicopters and the airplanes, she had heard the gunfire and the explosions, but the Americans had already left by the time she got there. All that remained was the destruction they had left behind. But she hadn't lost hope. Whoever had been there wasn't there for her. She had left a message for Jack, a message she still didn't have any way of knowing whether he had even received let alone acted upon, but she had to have faith.

And that was all that drove her now. Her nerves were a wreck, her tears spent, her chest aching from the sobs that had consumed her since her father's death.

She was nearing her end.

"Stop!"

She yelped but kept going, pretending to have not heard the command, her scrambled brain not making the connection that her utterance had revealed the fact she had indeed heard the order. Two shots rang out behind her and she squeezed her eyes shut as she applied pressure to the brake. It was over. She came to a halt and two soldiers ran up, one of them standing in front of her, blocking her path.

"What are you doing here?"

She had rehearsed what to say but couldn't form the words.

The man slapped her cheek hard. "I asked you a question! What are you doing here?"

Her eyes found fresh tears. "I'm scared! I'm just trying to get away from all the shooting!"

"Then why are you riding *toward* the shooting?"

"I don't know. I'm not thinking straight."

Someone walked up behind her. "What's going on here? Who is she?"

She cringed. She recognized the voice. It was the captain from earlier.

"What's your name?" he demanded.

Her entire body trembled. "Chesa," she lied.

"Turn around."

She kept her chin pressed to her chest but did as told, her eyes staring at the ground. A hand darted out and gripped her chin, yanking her face up.

"Eindra, we've been looking for you. Where's your father?"

More tears. "He's dead. He's dead because of you!"

The captain chuckled. "Because of me? I thought you said an American hit him in the head. I don't think I was born in America."

His men snickered. She didn't care anymore. She was dying regardless, so she might as well speed it up.

"It's people like you, people with those red scarves who think they can do anything they want to anybody they want with no consequences, it's you who killed my father!"

He sneered at her. "We don't *think* we can do anything we want, we *know* we can." He jerked at the scarf tied around his neck. "This gives me the license to do whatever I want, and there's nothing you could do or say to stop that." He let go of her chin and grabbed her by the neck, lifting her off the scooter. She struggled against the iron grip, her hands uselessly attempting to pry his fingers from her throat. "I'm going to ask you one more time. Who hit your father?"

She was about to black out and he eased up. She gasped for breath and gave in, her instinctual will to live kicking in. "One of your men did. Then the American shot your men before they could rape me."

The captain pushed her away, his eyes roaming her body. "What a great idea." He shoved her into the arms of one of his men. "Put her in my vehicle but don't touch her. I've got some energy I want to work off tonight."

The man gripping her by both shoulders sniffed her hair. "Can we have her when you're done, sir?"

The captain grunted as he turned away. "Only if you like screwing a corpse."

USS Ronald Reagan

Bay of Bengal

Dawson stepped onto the deck of the USS Ronald Reagan as a Viper launched nearby. He glanced over at it and his eyes narrowed as he spotted Jack in the pilot seat.

"Where the hell's he going?" asked Niner.

Dawson activated his comms. "Control, Zero-One. Where is Jackrabbit going, over?"

"Zero-One, Control, he's tying up a loose end."

"What kind of loose end?"

"A girl who helped Red and Sweets has requested extraction."

Red turned at the mention of his name and pointed at his ear. "Did I just hear what I think I heard?"

Dawson held up a finger. "Control, request permission to be redeployed to assist in the extraction, over."

"Negative, Zero-One. Your team is to stand down."

Dawson turned to the pilot of the Super Huey they had just stepped out of. "Do you have enough fuel for one more trip?"

The pilot checked. "I do, why?"

"Fire it back up, we're heading out." Dawson reactivated his comms. "Control, Zero-One. We're deploying now. I suggest you make it an order, otherwise you're going to be filling out my court-martial paperwork."

"Mine too," said Red, activating his comms.

"And mine," boomed Atlas.

"And mine." The team stepped forward as a whole.

Dawson smiled. "That girl and her father risked their lives to save one of ours and to provide shelter to Sweets. We *are* going to help her, over."

"Stand by, Zero-One."

Dawson pointed at Red, Niner, Atlas, Spock, and Jimmy. "You're with me. The rest of you, weapons and supplies, give them up then reequip yourselves and be prepared to come in and finish the job if shit goes bad." Mags, weapons, body armor, and other sundry items were handed over before Dawson and the others climbed in the back of the chopper. He leaned forward to talk to the pilot. "Have you got clearance?"

"Not yet."

Dawson cursed and was about to activate his comms when Leroux's voice cut in. "Zero-One, Control, you're a go. Try not to get yourselves killed. Believe it or not, that's even more paperwork, over."

Dawson chuckled as the pilot gave a thumbs-up, tapping his headset, indicating he had received clearance. Dawson sat beside Red as they lifted off. "Control, Zero-One. We'll try our best. Zero-One, out."

Operations Center 3, CIA Headquarters
Langley, Virginia

Leroux watched as Jack's Viper reached the coastline and hovered over the area where Eindra had indicated she would be, but there was nobody there.

"Control, Jackrabbit. Do you have eyes on her, over?"

"Negative, Jackrabbit."

"She said she'd be on a red scooter. Do you see anyone on a scooter?"

"Everyone in your immediate vicinity is on foot. We have soldiers just north of you, near Zero-One's extraction point. There are not a lot of civilians in the area."

"I've got something just to the north where those soldiers are," said Tong. The drone image zoomed in. "It's not a red scooter, it's a blue one. It's just sitting there abandoned, but look at that jeep nearby. Isn't that a girl sitting in the back?"

Leroux peered at the image. It was definitely a woman. "We need a shot of her face."

"Review the footage, see if you can find one," ordered Tong.

"Forget that." Leroux changed frequencies. "Drone Control, this is Command. Give the engine on drone Zulu Four-Two a rev, please."

"Roger that, Command. Revving now."

The girl looked up at the changed sound overhead and Tong grinned. "Got her." The isolated image expanded on the display.

"Get that to Jack." He switched his frequency back. "Jackrabbit, Control. We're sending you an image now. Confirm this is your target, over."

"Stand by, Control…Confirmed, Control. That's my girl. Is there any way I can get to her?"

Tong turned to Leroux, shaking her head. "There's no freaking way he's getting in there with a helicopter. Every gun there will be on him."

"Delta's ETA?"

"Five minutes. He's going to have to wait."

Leroux pointed at the tactical display showing the units in the area returning to base. "She might not have five minutes."

South of Yangon, Myanmar

Eindra sat in the back seat of the open-air army truck as one of the soldiers stood nearby, cackling about what would happen to her when they returned to base. She wept silently. She would be beaten and tortured and raped, then finally killed. She couldn't let that happen. She had to kill herself first, though she wasn't sure how to accomplish that. As she thought about it, she realized her best bet was to get killed rather than try to kill herself.

Somebody shouted nearby. "Captain Champo, we have orders to return to base."

Champo, the man who had been pursuing her father, acknowledged the report. This could be her last chance. She lunged forward and grabbed the knife off her guard's belt.

"Hey, what do you think—"

She shoved the blade into his stomach and twisted, just like she had seen in the movies. He cried out, grasping at the hilt. She scrambled into the driver's seat and started the vehicle, putting it in gear and hammering on the gas, thanking her late grandfather for having taught her how to drive at a young age, despite her insistence it was a skill she'd never need since she would never afford a car.

The truck jerked forward and she almost stalled it out as she struggled to shift into second. It had been years since she had been behind the wheel, but she managed to get it into gear and floored it, cranking the wheel to the left, heading away from the soldiers. Gunfire erupted behind her and she ducked, swerving around debris from the American attack, and directed herself south toward where Jack was expecting her. She didn't know if she could make it, but she didn't care. If she didn't, she was certain she would die trying.

Far preferable to the alternative she faced.

Jack pushed the stick forward, shaking his head with an appreciative smile at the latest update from Leroux. "That's my girl!" he cheered. She had managed to take out the soldier guarding her then steal the jeep. It completely changed the equation, but only if she could get far enough away from the ground forces still controlling the area.

He had to give her some help.

He raced along the ground, gaining enough altitude so he'd have coverage of the entire area, then spotted a jeep racing toward him, swerving madly, the driver clearly not experienced. At least half a dozen vehicles were in pursuit by drivers who knew what they were doing and they were rapidly closing the gap. He launched two Hellfire air-to-ground missiles, the rockets racing over Eindra's head, taking out the two closest pursuers.

She waved up at him as he blasted past, his cannons opening up on the scattered forces as he banked to his left, sweeping the entire area. He glanced back to see that she was still heading for the water. "Good girl. Don't stop, whatever you do."

He pulled a rapid 180, firing two more missiles that sent the ground troops scattering for cover as he squeezed more bursts from his cannons. He banked back toward the ocean, confident she had put enough of a gap between her and her pursuers for him to cover her. He pushed forward, gaining speed, and soon overtook her. He nosed up, killing his momentum then landed with a hard bounce as she skidded to a halt ten yards away.

He threw open the canopy and stood, beckoning to her. "Come on, let's go, let's go!"

She climbed out and stared at him. "Jack?"

He nodded, realizing she had never seen his face. "Yes, it's me. We met in your father's shop earlier today where I took my friend's body. Let's go before they get here!"

She sprinted toward him as gunfire opened up on them. He cursed as a technical crested the ridge, a .50 cal firing wildly as the gunner struggled to recover his balance.

And once he did, this rescue operation was over.

Champo jumped in the back of one of the few remaining vehicles that had survived the attack. "Let's go, let's go!"

One of his men dove into the driver's seat and fired up the engine, gunning them toward the ridge just ahead. The girl they had been after had escaped, but there was no way in hell he was letting her live. This was his last chance at revenge and he was determined to get it. They burst over the ridge and he was already squeezing the trigger, firing blindly ahead in the hopes that a stray bullet might catch the chopper's blades. They hit the ground hard, throwing him off balance, his hands still gripping the trigger, firing rounds wildly about. He slowly regained his balance and prepared to aim again as he spotted the helicopter ahead on the ground, the girl racing toward it.

She had to die. The pilot had to die.

Somebody had to die.

His niece was dead. His brother was dead. His men were dead. Countless countrymen were dead. But only two American soldiers were. The price in blood had to be higher than that, and he swore that if they got away, he would fulfill his bloodlust. He would make it his life's mission to kill every American he could. The embassy would reopen one day, the staff would return, and he would plot his revenge until then. And one day, he and his men would scale those walls and slaughter every single one of the bastards responsible for the death of his niece. If he had to, he'd fly to America and slit the throat of the ambassador's wife while her husband watched.

Blood would be spilled, far more than had been so far. Two American souls were not enough. Hundreds of Americans had to die, and right now he had a chance to exact some revenge and add to the toll.

He took aim at the chopper when somebody shouted to his left. He glanced over and his eyes narrowed.

"Who the hell is that?"

Aynslee sprinted toward the gunfire and explosions. She could hear a helicopter but not see it. Smoke billowed just ahead and she knew she was close. It had to be the Burmese fighting the Americans. There was no other possible explanation. She had to get to that battle and be seen by the right people, which could prove foolish since the wrong people were likely to see her as well. She rounded a long retaining wall and skidded to a halt at the carnage in front of her.

An attack helicopter that she had heard referred to as a Viper by one of the Special Forces team was strafing a Burmese position. Several vehicles were aflame as the chopper appeared to be protecting a jeep racing away from the scene, and Aynslee was surprised to see a young woman behind the wheel look back with terror in her eyes as she fled the mayhem. There had been talk about a girl and her father helping recover the dead soldier's body, and she had to wonder if this was that girl.

Whoever it was didn't matter right now. Whoever was in that helicopter had to see her if she had any hope of escaping. She took advantage of the distraction the pilot was providing and skirted the periphery of the battle zone, running as fast as she could, not bothering to check to see if she had been spotted. If she had been, the faster she moved, the less likely it was she would get hit.

There was a slight rise ahead that the jeep had disappeared over. If she could make it there then she just might get out of sight of all the guns to her right. She reached the top of the rise as the helicopter backed away, which was when someone took notice of her. There was a shout then gunfire, the dirt to her side erupting in small bursts. She dove to the ground and rolled head over heels down the side of the embankment. She winced as her shoulder slammed into a large rock, but she ignored it and shoved to her feet, continuing forward, the helicopter landing just ahead. The girl in the jeep sprinted toward it and it appeared she was going to make it.

But you're not.

An engine revved to her right and an enemy vehicle surged over the ridge, bouncing hard. A man firing a large gun from the rear was jostled about, and she stared in horror as the driver regained control.

Her prediction was entirely wrong.

The girl wasn't going to make it.

Whoever was manning the chopper reached out with a hand and pulled the girl into the front seat, but there wouldn't be time for him to lift off.

She had to do something.

She raised her hands in the air, waving her arms. "Hey, over here! Hey, asshole! Over here!"

The driver of the enemy vehicle didn't hear her, but the gunner did, taking a moment to glance over at her rather than fire on the chopper. The canopy closed on the Viper and she ran toward the enemy vehicle, still waving her hands. "Shoot me, asshole! I'm the one you want!" She doubted the man understood a word she was saying, but she had distracted him enough that the girl was safely inside the helicopter and perhaps there was a remote chance they could get away.

The gunner regained his focus and turned his attention back to the helicopter as it lifted off, his weapon belching deadly lead once again.

The driver slammed on the brakes, bringing them to a rapid halt so that his companion could aim better. Jostled once again, the man standing in the back had to recover yet again. Aynslee raced toward him, shouting and waving her arms in an attempt to buy a few more precious seconds.

She drew the attention of the driver and she gasped as a handgun appeared. Gunfire erupted from behind her and she hit the dirt then spun around to see a second helicopter banking toward her, muzzle flashes from the open side door pouring lead on the enemy vehicle. She rolled back onto her stomach and pushed up on her elbows to see the driver and gunman shredded to pieces. The Viper with the girl was now in the air and the second chopper pulled up then landed, the Special Forces team rushing out, two of them racing toward her.

She recognized Niner and Atlas and rose to her feet as they each grabbed her by an arm and hurried her back toward the chopper, the Viper now providing cover overhead, its weapons opening fire on the unseen enemy on the other side of the rise.

"Ms. Kai, you really should check your travel guide. If you want to find a good beach, Myanmar isn't exactly on anyone's list," cracked Niner.

Aynslee smiled, realizing what she had come to admire about these men she had only spent a couple of hours with. They were just normal guys who had decided to serve their country rather than lay bricks or work a desk. They were the best at what they did, but they were also human. They weren't automatons who blindly followed orders. They were funny, loving, caring men who put their lives on the line every day, not only for their country, but for those at home waiting for their son, their husband, their boyfriend, their father, to return home to them safely.

And as she scrambled into the back of the chopper, quickly followed by those who had put their lives on the line to save her when it had been made clear to her earlier that they wouldn't, she swore that when she told this story, it would be their humanity, not heroics, that would be made known to the American public.

Pope Field

Fort Bragg, North Carolina

Dawson gripped the handle of the casket, his chest tight, his eyes burning as he gave the order to proceed. Red was opposite him, at the front of the casket, those commanding Sweets on the mission leading the way. Niner, Atlas, Casey, and Jagger completed the group of pallbearers, and they made their way down the ramp of the C-5 Galaxy and into the sunlight of a warm North Carolina day.

The mission had been completed three days ago. The casualties had been light on their side, though no less painful to those who had lost a loved one. Devon Crane, the embassy driver, was the first to die, then Marsha Doyle the next night. Gunny Lee Daily was killed by the chopper blade, then Sergeant Donald "Sweets" Peters was the last American to die. According to the young Burmese woman, Eindra, her father had also died at the hands of the soldiers for having helped Red.

Too many had died, all because of an accident, the most tragic death the little girl who had innocently run out into traffic like so many kids did every day around the world. An innocent mistake made by a child, then an impulsive mistake made by an adult who ignored protocol, killing hundreds. Enemy casualties were heavy, very heavy, and it was unfortunate, but he never regretted killing an enemy firing at him.

The Myanmar government was blaming a Captain Champo for the carnage, apparently the uncle of the girl killed, and a member of the military who wore the red scarf. He commanded a unit big enough to trigger the chaos, despite orders handed down by his senior officers to let the rescue at the embassy go unchallenged. The Myanmar military knew what the response would be if they resisted after what had happened the night before, and they couldn't afford to lose more hardware.

Washington had demanded he stand trial, but photos were sent of his corpse. Eindra had identified the man as the one in charge of the troops that had killed her father, word of this fact just reaching them before they landed, which had put them in slightly better spirits. The man ultimately responsible for Sweets' death had paid the price, killed by one of Dawson's team as Champo fired a .50 cal from the rear of a jeep in an attempt to take down the Viper flown by Jack, and containing the girl that had become the demented man's focus for revenge.

Dawson just wished they had known who they were killing so they could have relished that fact sooner.

But now they had a job to do, and as they loaded the body into the back of the hearse, his heart was heavy. He had lost men before and it would never get easy, but this one was tough. Sweets had died saving Dawson's best friend, and part of him naturally was thankful that Red had survived, but he felt guilty that a very small part of him was happy they had lost Sweets and not Red.

His team was on standdown for now. One week off. A replacement would be brought in for Sweets, he would be integrated into the team, and in time, he would become a good friend just as Sweets had been. Sweets would never be forgotten, but he would be put out of mind and only acknowledged when all the fallen were, for dwelling on each individual death for too long was soul-crushing.

The hearse pulled away, the honor guard and his team saluting before Colonel Clancy dismissed them. Their commanding officer walked over and they all saluted. Clancy returned it then pointed at a nearby hangar. "Gentlemen, none of you are in proper attire. Go inside and change."

Dawson stared at his CO. "Sir?"

"You have one more mission today, Sergeant Major, and considering who gave the orders, there's no way in hell I'm letting you get away with not completing it."

Dawson's shoulders slumped. He was in no mood for a fourth mission without any downtime. He just wanted to go home, lay in bed, and fall asleep in Maggie's arms. The massive hangar doors slowly slid open, revealing wives and girlfriends, all wearing dresses. "What the hell's going on?"

Red slapped him on the back as the others gathered around him, laughing and smiling, all apparently in on the joke that he had been left out of.

"You're getting married, dude," grinned Atlas as they half-led, half-carried him toward the hangar.

302

The rest of the afternoon was a whirlwind. They had all changed into tuxes, then transports took them to the softball diamond behind the Unit where he had first discovered Maggie had feelings for him. Clancy had married them, which was absolutely perfect, and photos had been taken, Maggie radiant in every way, her hair she had been so concerned about after getting shot in the head, exquisite.

When all the formalities were over and the dinner began, he sat at one of the picnic tables set up and gave her a kiss. "How did you pull this off?"

She waved her hand at the Better Halves Club. "It was actually Shirley's idea, but once they heard, they all chipped in. We almost didn't have it when we found out about Sweets, but Lisa insisted that we go through with it." Her voice cracked. "Because that's what Sweets would've wanted."

Heads bobbed around all the tables in agreement. Maggie rose, taking Dawson's hand. "For those of you who might not be aware, Sweets earned his nickname because of his love of a certain type of food. This is why there's no choice between chicken or fish today."

"Today, everyone eats dessert!" shouted Vanessa as she rounded the corner carrying a platter, followed by a dozen catering staff provided by the base. She placed the platter down on the table in front of them then lifted the lid, revealing an assortment of homemade pastries and chocolates, a feast Sweets would have been ecstatic about.

Dawson rose, clapping hard as the rest of the team did the same. Tears flowed but smiles spread as this unit, this family, celebrated not only their nuptials, but the life of a fallen comrade.

Rest in peace, my brother.

THE END

ACKNOWLEDGMENTS

While working on this book, I heard the sad news that Angela Lansbury had died. One of my favorite shows has always been Murder, She Wrote. I used to watch it as a child, imagining myself a writer, keeping my latest manuscript in a leatherbound folder. To this day, I still watch the show, and it still brings a smile.

And the question: why the hell didn't anybody notice that Cabot Cove was the murder capital of the United States?

I've always wanted to be a writer, in part because of Angela Lansbury's Jessica Fletcher, and am fortunate to be living my dream thanks to readers like you.

As usual, there are people to thank. My dad for all the research, Ian Kennedy for some explosives info, Brent Richards for some military terminology, Michèle Easey for some canine info, and, as always, my wife and daughter, my late mother who will always be an angel on my shoulder as I write, as well as my friends for their continued support, and my fantastic proofreading team!

To those who have not already done so, please visit my website at www.jrobertkennedy.com, then sign up for the Insider's Club to be notified of new book releases. Your email address will never be shared or sold.

Thank you once again for reading.

Made in the USA
Middletown, DE
11 February 2023

24633727R00189